Lisa Worthey Smith

The Elijah Mandate

Plunged into danger.

Facing down the enemy.

Praying for a miracle.

A political conspiracy thriller
by bestselling and award-winning author,
Lisa Worthey Smith

Kerysso Press

Lisa Worthey Smith

Scripture quotations taken from the New American Standard Bible® (NASB),
Copyright © 1960, 1962, 1963, 1968, 1971, 1972, 1973,
1975, 1977, 1995 by The Lockman Foundation
Used by permission. www.Lockman.org

This book is partly biblical fiction—based on the true story of Elijah in 1 and 2 Kings—and partly a work of fiction. Names, characters, places, and incidents either are products of the author's imagination or are used fictitiously. Other than the story of Elijah, any resemblance to actual persons, living or dead, events, or locales is entirely coincidental.

Lisa Worthey Smith
Visit my website at www.LisaWortheySmith.com

KeryssoPress.blogspot.com

Printed in the United States of America

First Printing: Sept 2020

A portion of the proceeds from the sale of each book goes to charity.

Christian Mystery & Suspense
Conspiracy Fiction
Political Suspense Thriller
Political Conspiracy

ISBN-13 978-1-7344954-6-1
ASIN-B08GVSC42S

Kerysso Press

Reviews

"Intrigue. Danger. A lot to lose. A lot to gain. Such is the plot of *The Elijah Mandate* revealing the creative writing and mind of Lisa Worthey Smith. Smith continues to produce award winning books which include significant messages of hope in God and trust in His plan. *The Elijah Mandate* draws you in and won't let you go. I was hooked early on."

KATHY COLLARD MILLER, author of over 50 books including *God's Intriguing Questions: 60 New Testament Devotions Revealing Jesus's Nature*

"Faith and values intertwined in a political thriller that will keep you turning the pages. Expertly compared to Eliana, Lisa Smith connected Elijah's biblical journey to a fictional, yet credible, story of today.

"I highly recommend this book! It is a must read for those who enjoy Christian thrillers and suspense."

SANDI HERRON, author

"Thought-provoking, exciting, and timely. The author wove history and present circumstances together in an amazing way. I'll be thinking about this one for a long time."

SHERRI STEWART, author

"Superb! A fast-paced political thriller based on Eliana, a modern-day Elijah. The web of deceit is spread far and wide, all the way up to the Supreme Court. Lisa Smith has skillfully woven an exciting and timely tale of deception and intrigue. The faith and obedience of both Elijah and Eliana are inspirational to us all."

T. HOLLAND

"WOW! I couldn't put this book down. The biblical story of Elijah set in the headlines of today kept me turning just one more page. I pray, along with Eliana, that God would 'Let my remaining days be fully and wholly dedicated to serving You, no matter the obstacles that seem overwhelming.'"

S. TILLEY

"Such an intriguing and thought-provoking book. Lisa Smith, using events in the life of the prophet Elijah, provides a deeper insight into our present societal circumstances. I had a hard time putting this book down!"

HANNAH CAMERON, educator

*Dedicated to all those
who mourn over the evil in the world,
who look to God for direction,
and to those who are equipping them
to complete their mandate,
no matter the cost.*

Lisa Worthey Smith

Preface

A nation turned its back on God, routinely sacrificed babies, drenched themselves in moral depravity, and trivialized their sins. Years ago, those practices described Israel. God used Elijah to remind that country of His sovereign authority.

Today, in the United States, similar sins run rampant. The call to eliminate God and continue in this "new normal," rings louder daily.

The Elijah Mandate weaves today's headlines and trends into a modern-day Elijah story, where God uses one girl to remind America of His sovereignty.

I pray this story provides a glimpse of how powerful and steadfast the God of Elijah and His Word remain today. It is my fervent prayer that you will seek Him, listen to Him, and allow Him to use you, perhaps in ways you never imagined.

Lisa

Ephesians 6:12 "For our struggle is not against flesh and blood, but against the rulers, against the powers, against the world forces of this darkness, against the spiritual forces of wickedness in the heavenly places."

Lisa Worthey Smith

The Elijah Mandate

By

Lisa Worthey Smith

Lisa Worthey Smith

Prologue

Forty-eight years earlier

On their wedding day, Eliana's grandparents, Milton and Patricia, waited in separate rooms at the church for the ceremony to begin. A mutual friend delivered the following note to the bride from the groom.

My dearest Patricia,

From the moment I heard you playing the organ at Harvard-Epworth United Methodist Church, I knew you were special. When I spoke to you after the service that Sunday, I hoped you wouldn't find this clumsy law student terribly offensive. To my great surprise and relief, you agreed to meet me on the Commons for lunch the following day. Our daily talks evolved into prayer sessions where we beseeched God to lead us to make decisions that glorified Him. Those talks and prayers only made me love you more.

I'm so thankful God led us to build our lives together. I count it a blessing from Him to have you by my side. You are a treasure beyond comparison, a gift from heaven.

Today, we meet again in the same church to be united as Mr. and Mrs. Moore. No matter what the days hold, I will be beside you to support you, to love and cherish you, and to work alongside you as we build a home filled with children, laughter, music, and love—a home, that will honor God above all.

As I eagerly await you joining me in holy matrimony before God and man, I send you this note with this pearl necklace. The pearls will fade in comparison to your beauty, but I send it as a token of my unending love for you,

Milton

~~

Milton, dearest,

I love you with all my heart, but I cannot possibly accept such an extravagant gift. Until you set up your practice, we will need that money for living expenses. I love you dearly, but must ask that you exchange this for something more practical.

I will see you at the end of the aisle. I will wear my smile filled with love, and look forward to seeing yours today and for years to come. Your smile is all I need.

Patricia.

~~

Patricia,

I reiterate my undying love but will not grant you this request. I will not return it for something practical any more than I would marry a wealthy girl to appease my parents. Let us begin our marriage with one extravagant gift and the prayer that God will grant us many years of extravagant love.

Milton

P.S. My smile awaits yours.

Lisa Worthey Smith

Chapter One

Eliana fingered the pearls around her neck while she waited for her turn to walk to the stage. The necklace, a symbol of her grandparents' extravagant love, would be with her for her law school graduation, even if they couldn't.

As she neared the steps to the platform, her cellphone buzzed in her hip pocket, but it would have to wait. Eliana checked the tassel on her mortarboard, stepped up to the stage, and strode toward the dean of the Law School to accept her diploma. She received the treasured Juris Doctor certificate with her left hand, exchanged a handshake with the dean with her right hand, and held the pose while the official photographer snapped a photo.

"Woohoo, Ellie. Way to go," a voice blasted from the audience.

She cringed, blushed, and hoped her brother wouldn't embarrass her with anything more than that. Her mother had probably already elbowed him for the outburst. Her brother—adorable, fun-loving, but still a little too loud and brash. *He'll grow out of it one day, I hope. Eventually. Surely one day it will happen.*

Her left hand clutched the leathery cover close to her heart, restraining the multitude of cords dangling from her neck from bouncing with every step. Head up, confidence beamed from Eliana's face with every stride. After years of study and work, her long-time dream of being a lawyer, finally became a reality. The only hurdle remaining, to pass the bar exam.

Brace yourself, world, here I come.

Her eyes brimmed with tears. *Daddy and Granddaddy would be so proud.* They both wanted her to go to law school and join them in their law practice, but Eliana begged her granddaddy to request a position for her with his college friend, Justice Abram, in the US Supreme Court.

He pretended that he would not, but I wouldn't be surprised if he did send a letter of recommendation to Abram before he died. At least I hope he did. It would be a place where I could make a difference, especially with the turmoil in the news every day.

While the names of other graduates echoed in the grand auditorium, another series of vibrations rumbled in her pocket. *How rude would it be to check the message, while the rest receive their diplomas? Come on. If not outright rude, at least disrespectful. They deserve my attention for their moment of recognition. It can wait.*

The woo-hoos rang out again at the end of the ceremony, and the new graduates congratulated one another and searched the crowd for their families. Through the chaos, Eliana heard her mother's sweet voice. "Honey, I am so proud of you."

Eliana turned to the side and into her mother's open arms.

"Your daddy and granddaddy would be so proud."

"I hope so, Mom. I couldn't help but wonder if they were able to look down and see this."

Her mother's chin trembled. She pressed her lips between her teeth. "I hope so, sweetheart. I really do. J.T. and Daddy loved you so."

"Great job, Sis." Johnny tossed her cords up in her face.

Eliana grabbed his hands to stop the nonsense. "Thanks. Heard you cheering for me."

"Had to cheer on my older sister. It's what brothers do."

"Really? I seem to remember—"

"Come on. I can't let you to get too much of a big head." He flopped her mortarboard from the back, pushing the front down into her eyes, then ducked in anticipation of retaliation.

"Johnny." Eliana reconsidered delivering the jab he deserved and smirked. "I love you, kiddo."

"Love ya too," Johnny added with a wink and that impish smile that allowed him to get away with far too much.

Their mother interrupted, "Come on, you two. Let's go celebrate."

"Sounds good to me." Johnny turned to leave. "Wait 'til you see the cake she made for you."

"Mom. You didn't have to do that. With all you've had to deal with these last few weeks—"

Her mother grabbed her hand. "I wanted to, sweetheart. I can't give you much, but I wanted this day to be as special as I could make it."

Eliana embraced her mother with a long deep hug for the strength and support she provided. Widowed years ago, Grace had just buried her father, Milton, a few weeks ago but still worked to make this day special for her daughter. "Mom, you being here for me all my life, not just today, makes it special. More special than you know."

~~

The guests at the graduation party oohed and ahhed when Eliana's mom paraded from the kitchen with the stunning cake, topped with the scales of justice. She added her confectionary creation to the dining table already teeming with finger foods. The well-wishers took turns congratulating Eliana, quizzing Johnny about his college options, and offering to do anything they could to help her mother. The blessing of friends overflowed in their home—this time with joy.

After everyone had their fill of cake and snacks, Eliana opened cards filled with heartfelt congratulations, money, and gift cards. When the crowd dwindled, she summoned Johnny to help her clean up so their mother could rest.

In the kitchen, the brother and sister reminisced about childhood memories and wished their dad could have seen the events of the day. The cancer had taken J.T. quickly, years ago, when Eliana was thirteen.

Their granddaddy, Milton, made sure they didn't lack anything. But a few weeks ago, a sudden heart attack took him, too. With both law firm partners gone, no one knew quite what to do about Moore and Barrington law firm. Their mother had worked as a secretary there most of her adult life. What would she do without that income?

Granddaddy always told me he left the Barrington name in the law firm after Daddy died, because he hoped I would join the practice after law school. I guess I could, after I pass the bar. I had hoped …

Eliana paused the conversation when she remembered her phone vibration earlier in the day. She pulled her cell out of her pocket, swiped it open, and turned up the volume. The notifications included two missed calls from a 202-area code, and one message. Eliana played the voice mail and leaned against the countertop.

"An admirer, sis?" Johnny perched on the counter, fluttered his eyelids, and fanned his face like a swooning Southern belle.

"Shh. It's important." Her eyes widened and her face flushed.

"What is it, Ellie?" Johnny frowned.

"Just a minute." She shifted the phone to her left ear and used her right hand to find a pencil and take notes.

When she pulled it back from her ear, she squealed. "I got the job. They want me to start by the first of the month. Your big sister is going to work for a Supreme Court justice. In D.C."

"Let's go tell Mom."

Johnny reached her first and jostled the back of her chair to rouse her from her nap.

"What?" Grace blinked at her wide-eyed children. "What's wrong?"

Eliana held out her phone and replayed the voicemail for her. Eliana and Johnny froze in place, watching their mother's expression while the message played.

Grace's eyes grew big, then teared as the voice requested Eliana to report to work. She clapped her hands. "What a blessing, dear child. You will be a wonderful asset to the justice and to the court. I'm so happy for you." She pulled Eliana's hands into hers and squeezed them. "God has heard and answered."

Johnny paused his happy dance and woo-hooing. "Can we turn her room into a workout room?"

Eliana put her hands on her hips. "You're headed to college in the fall yourself. Leave my room alone."

Grace interrupted, "God gave you both to me, and I will always have room for my babies here. As a matter of fact, I might bring out the baby pictures and—"

"Mom. Please. No." Johnny rolled his eyes.

"You do what you want, Mom. I'll keep Johnny in line. Somebody has to."

"You know that's God's job. I'm counting on Him to keep you both in line. You both had better keep in mind whose you are and whose name you carry, wherever you go."

Johnny leaned near Eliana and whispered, "Here comes the righteousness speech," then shuffled away from them. "Think I'll go plan my workout room while you two summon the power of God to eliminate all evil from the world."

"Don't you want to be in on the plan?" Eliana asked.

"I got it already. Where have you been?" Johnny waved to them as he left the room.

~~

In Eliana's first few days in the nation's capital, she found an apartment in a safe area, obtained her security card from human resources, then took a tourist tour to get her bearings in the Supreme Court building. This Greek style "temple of the law" boasted huge Alabama marble spiral staircases and massive bronze doors on the western entrance which led into the courtroom. Whole forests must have been depleted of mahogany to fill these rooms with furniture and paneling. The tour guide announced that the designers intended the elaborate setting to showcase the grandeur of the law.

At her 1:00 p.m. meeting with Justice Abram, he welcomed her with a hearty handshake and spoke of her granddaddy in glowing terms. "I see Milton in your eyes. It will be like seeing him when I see you here. Milton Moore was a good man, a good lawyer, and a good friend. I'm glad to have you here. My secretary, Julie, will show you around. As you know, the clerks will gather case law, but your job will be to gather information on a variety of topics. If you have any questions, feel free to ask one of the clerks."

"Thank you, sir. It is a great honor to be here and to get to know one of my granddaddy's friends. I will do my very best."

~~

Monday 7:30 a.m.
Eliana had brought her bicycle to the city for commuting around town, but until she found out if she had a place to park it at work, a taxi would be her best option for her first day.

She gave the clasp on her pearls a good push, and then tugged them to ensure they were secure. Eliana looked at herself in the mirror and fingered the necklace that landed just below her collarbone. *Granddaddy, I wish you could see me. Wearing her pearls. Working for Justice Abram. Thank you for always paving the way for me. I'll tell Grandma about it when I see her. You tell Daddy for me.*

Eliana imagined seeing her daddy and granddaddy in the reflection, standing behind her. The recent sudden loss of her granddaddy only refreshed the pain of losing her daddy.

The two most important men in her life had been partners in Moore and Barrington, and in loving Eliana. They each loved her unconditionally and made sure she knew it. Even though their reflection only shone in her imagination, their presence within her was real.

J.T. adored his little girl and playfully called her his "Ellie Belle." Milton, her granddaddy, called her "Ana." Not "Anna"— rhyming with Hannah—as most of her friends called her, and not "Ellie" as her stubborn brother called her. With his baritone voice— smooth as French silk—Granddaddy called her, "Ahhna," as if it were the most beautiful name in all the earth. His voice could boom to every corner of a courtroom, but with her, his voice always had a breathy softness, uniquely his own.

Now, it would be up to Eliana Barrington to carry on their legacy in the next generation of attorneys.

The mirror revealed that her hemline reached a respectable length. *Good.* But her neckline dipped a little lower than she thought proper, so two safety pins at the shoulders lifted it up to a more modest placement. *Don't want to give the wrong impression on my first day.*

Eliana gave one more pat to the pearls and said a quick prayer. She gulped the final swallow of coffee in her mug, draped the lanyard with her security card around her neck, and headed out the door.

The taxi delivered her in a timely manner, but it took longer than she expected to navigate the busy halls and elevators. By the time she reached the second-floor justice chambers, she only had five minutes to spare, late by her reckoning.

When she pushed open the door to Justice Abram's office, his secretary, Julie, glanced at the ornate walnut grandfather clock, pulled a chair alongside her own desk, and motioned to it. "Good morning. This is a busy time of day. Why don't you sit here and become acquainted with the activities and the personnel in the office? He has requisitioned a desk for you to sit alongside mine. It should be here by the end of the day. We'll talk more in a little while."

Clerks popped in and out of Abram's office, always glancing at the grandfather clock. Julie tapped the daily planner open on the corner of her desk, the old-fashioned kind made of paper and lines. She explained that from 10:00 a.m. until noon, on Mondays, Tuesdays, and Wednesdays, the court held two arguments each lasting one hour. The court held no public sessions Thursdays and Fridays, and the justices used that time to meet about the cases argued and to discuss and vote on petitions for review.

Julie announced each clerk, Ron, Kirstie, Matt, and Shally, as they came in and pointed to Eliana, introducing her as a recent law school graduate who would be conducting special research for Justice Abram.

When the justice opened his office door, the clerks buzzed around him, giving him last-second files and information. As he led the parade of clerks out of his office, Abram nodded toward Eliana, and headed to the hallway leading to the courtroom. Within a minute, the clock's Westminster chime rang out ten o'clock, and Julie's office quieted.

"Want to listen?" Julie stood.

"Yes ma'am."

Julie's eyes hardened. "Drop the 'ma'am.' I'm Julie."

Eliana nodded and shadowed her down the hall. Julie put her finger in front of her lips and stood motionless.

Inside the courtroom, the marshal announced, "The Honorable, the Chief justice and the Associate justices of the Supreme Court of the United States. Oyez! Oyez! Oyez! All persons having business before the Honorable, the Supreme Court of the United States, are admonished to draw near and give their attention, for the Court is now sitting. God save the United States and this Honorable Court!"

Eliana touched her pearls and looked to the ceiling. *Oh, how I wish you could see this.*

Julie tugged at Eliana's sleeve, "Pretty special, huh? Let's go back to the office. I'll show you the docket and the petitions to be reviewed, so you can get an idea of the topics you might need to research."

"I'm sorry I was late this morning."

"You weren't late. Just plan to allow a little more time, so you can get settled before eight o'clock."

"Do you know if I'm allowed to bring a bicycle and park it in the garage? My apartment is so close, it would be convenient if I could."

"I think you are. Check with security for a parking pass and see what they say."

"Thanks. I will." While Julie tapped at the keyboard, Eliana thumbed through a stack of files. The docket included arguments ranging from gun restriction to school policies, whether evidence may be used in trial, whether a person's right to privacy had been abused, whether malice was at issue for intent, whether cruel and unusual punishment was at issue, whether some religious services might violate laws, and whether prayer should be allowed at certain venues.

Eliana had argued some of these topics in mock trials. *This will be fun. A great opportunity to bring the truth to the forefront and provide an alternative viewpoint from the political action committees who bombard the house and the senate with propaganda that suited their interests. I can't wait to tell Mom.*

Julie finished her morning notes and turned to check on Eliana. "Afternoons consist of conferences about the recently argued cases and topics of interest to Justice Abram. 'Elianna,' is that how you pronounce your name? This is when you will interact with Justice Abram."

"Eliana or 'Ana.' My mother is the only one who calls me by my full name. When I hear 'Eliana,' it still makes me think I'm in trouble."

Julie laughed. "'Ana' it is then."

Eliana patted the stack of papers before her and asked, "Do you know what case he currently needs information on?" *Great. First day and already forgetting all grammar. It should have been 'on which case he needs information.' Now she'll think I am totally inadequate.*

Julie shook her head. "He'll let you know what he wants, probably after lunch."

The chime at noon brought another flurry of activity as the staff clamored to scarf down their lunch in their third-floor dining area designated for Justice Abram. A perk of the job included free access to the catered buffet of sandwiches, pizzas, chicken tenders, and other hearty finger foods. Abram's staff gathered at a table with the justice. Julie motioned her to join in.

Eliana pulled a chicken salad sandwich plate and some chips from the buffet. She filled her cup with Dr. Pepper and balanced it under the plate. With two fingers, she picked up a few napkins and joined the group at the table.

When everyone settled at the table, Abram introduced her with a summary of her scholastic achievements and her father's and grandfather's law practice, ending with a mention of the friendship he shared with Milton Moore, her grandfather. "We met at Harvard Law School. Milton was brilliant. Probably one of the most brilliant legal minds I ever met. He had the jury eating out of his hand, and convincing them that only a judgment in favor of his client made any sense at all. Just brilliant."

Abram turned to Eliana, "I didn't know your father, J.T., but I talked with Milton when the cancer hit him. I was very sorry to hear of his passing. Your grandfather said Moore and Barrington was a nice small-town practice. Milton always represented his clients with integrity." Abram pursed his lips and tapped his fingers together to make his concluding statement. "Brilliance with integrity. That sums up Milton Moore."

Eliana nodded at the kind words. *God, help me to live up to that standard in my own legal career. Maybe someday, someone will say that about me.*

Julie nibbled at her lunch. While Abram updated the attentive clerks on the arguments of the morning, he added a few remarks about how nicely a female attorney "filled out her business suit" at the second hearing. He caught Julie's eye and asked her to send the contact information for the "suit" to him that afternoon. Julie nodded and continued her dainty bites.

The clerks snickered at his innuendos, roared in hearty laughter at his jokes, and nodded at his every comment about the cases. Some copied his lunch menu, gestures, and word choices. Abram obviously reigned as supreme king over the groupies seated at his table.

When Abram finished his lunch, Shally leaned toward the justice to reach his empty plate. A strand of her long curls tapped him on his shoulder, and he glanced in her direction, his gaze lingering on the space between the buttons of her blouse that stretched to their limit.

"Excuse me, sir." Shally drawled and stretched farther across him to reach his cup, brushing against him.

"You're excused." Their knowing smiles unnerved Eliana and she lowered her head to hide the flush of her cheeks at the open flirtation. She stacked her throwaways and topped the pile with her napkins.

When Shally left and Eliana rose, Abram called to her, "Eliana. I have a case before me about church sermons and broadcasts—freedom of speech, and hate speech. I always counted on Milton to be my conscience in such matters, and I want you to round up some information for me. The clerks will look for legal precedents, but I want to explore a wider range of information."

"Of course, sir."

~~

Monday evening
5:45 p.m.

Eliana tossed the keys in a bowl by the front door, and plopped in a chair to call her mom. "I applied for a parking pass today, so I can ride my bike to work. They brought in a desk for me to sit by his secretary. She's perfect, proper, and efficient. Abram's clerks practically bow in worship to him, and are constantly vying for his favor, but he said something interesting. He told me he thought of Granddaddy as his conscience and implied it had to do with things like religious matters. Did he ever talk to you about that?"

"Only vaguely, dear. Your grandfather tried to talk with him about godly things, but Abram was somewhat resistant to hearing them. To his credit, though, he did seek opinions of people who took their faith seriously. I'm glad he has you there. You will give him sound information. God has you right where He wants to use you so that others will know He is God."

"Yeah, I know. The Elijah thing."

"Well, it's true. It's what He told me about you before you were born. If you had been a boy, I would have named you Elijah. But I used the feminine equivalent—Eliana, meaning "My God answered.""

"You really thought I would be a boy?"

"I didn't have a promise about that. Just that He would use you like he did Elijah. Boy or girl doesn't matter. He plans to use you. He told me, and I believe it. Besides, I'm your mom. I know these things."

"Love you, Mom."

"I love you too, sweetheart. Thanks for calling. Bye."

Dear Mom. She never gets tired of telling that story.

~~

Tuesday
7:45 a.m.

A well-dressed woman was coming out of Abram's office buttoning her blouse with one hand and clutching an expensive leather satchel with the other as Eliana came into the outer office to her new desk.

"Good morning," Eliana chirped.

"Morning," she murmured with raised eyebrows. She turned to face the mirror by the door and lifted a few strands of hair into place. While her French manicured hands smoothed her skirt, Eliana read the elaborate script embossed on her satchel. "Social Justice and Equalization Foundation."

The woman smiled at her reflection, apparently satisfied she was presentable, opened the door, and clicked her Louboutin heels down the marble hall without any further acknowledgement of Eliana.

Julie popped her head in with a cheery "good morning. I guess we didn't scare you too much yesterday. You came back."

Eliana decided not to mention the woman, at least for the moment. *No point in starting on the wrong foot. I really don't know why she was here. It could be perfectly innocent.*

"I saw Cheryl Markham coming from this direction. Did you meet her?"

Eliana stuttered, "There was a woman—"

"Louboutins?"

Eliana nodded.

Julie took a deep breath, "That's Cheryl. You will see her here from time to time."

Eliana waited for more explanation, but none came.

Julie flipped pages, shuffled folders and prepared for the morning frenzy.

When the ten o'clock court session began and they had the office to themselves, Julie caught her eye. "A word of advice."

"Sure."

"Ana, you came from a small town, and I appreciate your modest dress and demeanor. I'm afraid you might not be acquainted with the way things are done here. Just do your job, and you will be fine."

"I will. Thank you." Eliana gave a nod of agreement. *Guess that explains Abram's early morning visitor.*

"Good. Let's get to work."

Eliana sat at her desk and looked through the freedom of speech case and the sermons in question. The nonstop phone calls prompted Eliana to ask Julie if it would be appropriate for her to work in the library on the fourth floor. It held vast volumes of case law, but with the availability of digitized legal precedents, the books in the library gathered more dust than fingerprints.

Julie agreed. "It's a quiet space and it should pose no problems for you to work there. If you need any help, Olivia is the librarian. She'll help you find what you need."

Eliana introduced herself to Olivia, chose a table in the far corner of the cavernous room with richly carved mahogany arches and ornate ceilings with massive chandeliers. While her laptop booted up, she slid her hand over the beautiful tabletop and took in the scene. *The Supreme Court library. Eliana Barrington is working for a United States Supreme Court justice in a place where so many law students dream of visiting.* Eliana rubbed the goosebumps on her arms. *I'd better put on a professional face before anyone walks in and sees my goofy grin and tries to toss me out as a straggling tourist.*

Clerks mostly worked in their third-floor offices and joined the justice at lunch for instructions or afternoon discussions. Ron, one of Abram's clerks, came into the library and took a seat close to Eliana.

Tall, slender, and filled with boyish charm, he spoke, "Hi, Eliana. We haven't had a chance to talk since you started here. Lunch is busy, and I guess you work on different cases than we do. Are you studying for the bar?"

"Right now? No. I do that at night within an online study group. I'm working on some research for Abram. Are you studying for the bar?"

"Of course. When I finish being errand boy for Abram, I pore over the books. Gotta get that checked off my list, then I'll apply to a firm here in D.C. One day I'll be a partner, raking in the dough with my name on the front door." He held up his arms, basking in the glory he had not yet fully achieved.

"Good for you. I'm sure you will do well." Eliana continued clicking on her keyboard.

"Oh, I will." He raised his eyebrows and smiled. "Do well, that is."

Eliana didn't raise her eyes to even acknowledge the innuendo. Instead, she focused on the computer screen.

Ron stood, pressed his palms on the table and leaned over Eliana. "Hey, want to go grab a drink after work? You know what 'all work' does."

Eliana shook her head. *Seems like a nice guy, but this really isn't the time or place for that.* "Thanks, Ron. I appreciate it, but I'll pass. I do need to study for the bar."

"Yeah. That online study group. Okay." He clapped his hands together and tossed his blond bangs to the side. "After a few more weeks here, you might need a drink. I'll check with you later." He winked at her and patted the desk as he left.

Within half an hour, Matt came and sat beside her. In contrast to Ron's boyish look, Matt had the brawn of a lumberjack but dressed in a custom-tailored Fifth Avenue suit. Dark hair framed his movie-star face. "Hi. Just wanted to see how you're coming along. Getting to know your way around?"

"Yes, I think so. Thanks."

He propped one arm on the table in front of them and twisted to lean closer to her face. "So, what are your plans? Politics? Private practice? Family firm?"

Eliana leaned back in her chair to regain a little personal space. "Actually, my daddy and granddaddy were in a practice together, but the office is closed now. My granddaddy died last month, and my daddy died several years ago."

"Wow. I'm sorry. That's tough."

"Thanks. It has been hard. With both of them gone, I don't know that I want to take on the practice alone. I haven't decided yet. I've always known I would go into law. I'm just praying God will show me what He wants me to do. What will you do next?"

"Me? Yeah, Supreme Court clerk has been a nice start, but I'm considering tossing my hat into the political ring. My family dabbles in politics. My dad was secretary of state in Georgia for several terms. He has a private practice now. One sister works here in D.C. She worked on the presidential campaign trail and settled into corporate law. Another sister is a state representative, but I expect she will run for a higher office soon. So, I have some options. I've gotten to know some of the movers and shakers up here—you know, contacts who will open doors and take me places." He lightly shrugged, as if he were thoroughly impressed with his pedigree and his future.

"Great. Sounds like you have it all planned out." Eliana tried to focus her brain on the research in front of her.

"Speaking of plans," Matt turned on the charm, "tell me, what does a gorgeous girl like you do for fun?"

Eliana chuckled. "Fun? You mean this isn't fun?"

Matt smiled a megawatt, Hollywood smile. "You know what I mean. After work. Leisure. Excitement. Sports. Harvard heavyweight rowing team here." He tapped his biceps. "Chess? What do you like to do in your playtime?"

Eliana looked at a vacant space above the computer screen. "Good question. I've spent so many years in the books, I really don't know. Right now, I am studying for the bar at night."

"Yeah, I heard you have an online study group."

The trusty workplace grapevine.

"But a girl can become lonely. You know what I mean?" He raised his shoulders in a plea.

This guy is used to dropping names, turning on the charm, and getting what he wants. I'm not here to start a workplace romance—they rarely end well—and he never acknowledged my comment about God.

"Matt." Eliana shook her head and looked at him, giving him her best polite but firm smile. "I'm not interested in anything but my job here, and passing the bar right now."

"Well, you know where I am if you change your mind." He winked and added, "When you change your mind."

"Thanks, Matt."

Lisa Worthey Smith

Chapter Two

Thursday

Markham came out of Abram's office right on time. Oblivious to Eliana, she stood in front of the mirror by the door. She wiped off some lipstick smudges and straightened her collar before she opened the door.

As her Louboutin heels clicked on their morning route, Abram opened his door and motioned toward her with a nod. "Come in. How much have you gathered about the freedom of speech and sermons case?"

Abram leaned on the corner of his desk and crossed his arms in front of him.

Eliana touched the strand of pearls around her neck and followed him into his chambers. Leaving the door open, she stood before him and began, "Justice Abram, I find this case very disturbing. I read the sermon and found nothing illegal in it. I read the transcript of the state trial and do not agree at all with their prosecution of the case. Their claims of political bias, undue influence, and coercion were completely without merit. The pastor simply urged the congregation to vote, and to vote according to biblical principles. He did not mention one party or another. I saw no malice, no intent to incite anyone, simply that they vote."

"What about using his position of influence over their vote?"

"He didn't threaten to monitor them in any way or even ask how they voted. He simply stated the biblical truth and pointed out the issues on the ballot."

"You do sound a lot like Milton."

"I take that as a compliment, Your Honor."

"You don't find it disturbing that this pastor exerts influence over his dimwitted followers?"

"Dim-witted, Your Honor?"

"You know how people are. They blindly follow preachers who promise health, wealth, and prosperity. That could easily be construed as undue influence and coercion. If they disappoint this religious leader, they might reasonably expect they would lose their health or he might cast some spell over them. If they break his rules, they could lose standing in the church."

"Your Honor, this sermon in question, neither offered a quid pro quo, nor did it imply any punishment or retaliation."

"But it came from the pulpit where he promotes his agenda in front of a captive audience without question. Is it not implied that going against the so-called rules of the church will earn punishment?"

"They were not captive, Your Honor, and it was not an agenda. It was a comparison of the issues on the ballot to what the Word of God had to say about those issues. There is punishment for going against the Word of God but not from the pastor. It comes from God Almighty Himself."

Abram's steely glare and silence after her last response sent chills up Eliana's spine and clenched her vocal cords.

She swallowed and cleared her throat. "Your Honor, he crossed no moral or legal boundaries with the sermon, including prompting the citizens within the congregation to vote. We all have a duty to vote and vote for what is right in God's eyes. He is God. We cannot leave Him out of our decision-making and expect to do the right thing."

"Thank you, Eliana, for you impassioned opinion. I will take it under consideration." He uncrossed his arms and motioned for her to leave.

~~

The justices met to deliberate the cases already argued and the petitions to be reviewed, then everyone met in the dining room for lunch. The four clerks all volleyed for Abram's attention.

When the justices returned to the conference room for deliberations, Ron and Matt huddled together while Kirstie and Shally cleaned up from lunch. The male clerks whispered and pointed at Kirstie as she sashayed out of the dining room as if she were the sole exhibition on the catwalk. When she reached the door, she turned to them and gave a wink, rousing muffled laughter from them both.

Eliana grunted at their sophomoric display, stuffed her napkin in her cup, set it on her plate, and left the table without a word. *I thought I left college antics at undergrad school. Two grown men ... grown women, acting like*—Eliana flinched when a hand tapped her shoulder, and she juggled to balance her plate.

"Oh, sorry. Didn't mean to startle you." Julie helped her catch the cup before it tumbled.

"Thanks. No problem. I just didn't see you there." Eliana stabilized her stack of trash.

Julie took in a breath. "I wanted to touch base with you." Julie glanced toward the giggling clerks. "The clerks engage in—"

"So, I see," Eliana interrupted.

Julie nodded. "There are a lot of high-powered people around here. Influencers. If you're in with the right people, you move up. If you offend the wrong people, you are blackballed. They—," Julie's eyes darted toward Ron and Matt, "are learning how to get ahead. Most are a little more subtle with their approach, but those two don't seem to care who knows."

"I appreciate the insight. I plan to stick with the old-fashioned way and let my work speak for itself."

"That's a noble approach. I admire that."

Eliana and Julie left the dining room and headed back to Justice Abram's office. "Julie, may I ask about you? I mean, I see your wedding rings, but you haven't mentioned your husband or children. I hope that's not too forward."

"I don't mind." Julie stretched out her left hand and gazed at her wedding rings. "I am married. My husband, Todd, served in the military and has severe Post Traumatic Stress Disorder, PTSD. He has a little woodworking shop and makes custom orders when he is able. We have a daughter, Emma, who is twelve, with special needs and requires full-time care at an expensive school."

"Wow. I didn't mean to pry. It sounds like you carry a lot on your shoulders."

"No problem. I don't broadcast it, but it's no big secret."

"I understand. I hope I can meet them sometime."

In front of them, Abram opened the door to the outer office for Shally, and he followed her in.

Eliana stopped and looked toward the closing door. "How do you handle seeing all the … private meetings … around here?"

Julie glanced at the door, grimaced, then whispered, "I just ignore it. I can't afford to lose this job. My family depends on the income and the insurance." She shook her head. "I'm not going to participate in it, but I can't risk the backlash if I report it, so I close my eyes to it, pretend I see nothing, and let it go."

The click of heels on the floor behind them ended the conversation. They walked into the office and returned to work, with Abram and Shally just yards away.

In his office.

Behind closed doors.

Julie pressed Abram's office intercom and announced, "Five minutes until conference, sir."

Within a minute, Shally emerged with her stack of folders, and Abram followed, brushing by them to hurry to his meeting. Shally hopped on the corner of Eliana's desk. When she sat, the slit in her skirt opened nearly to her hip bone. Near the top of the slit, Eliana caught a glimpse of a tattooed heart on her thigh, pierced with Cupid's arrow, the bottom half of some calligraphy above the heart. "So, how do you like working here so far, Ellie Ann?"

"Eliana, or Ana. I like it a lot, thank you. 'Shelly', is it?"

"'Shalom,' actually. I usually go by 'Shally.' Working on anything or anyone interesting?" Shallie wiggled her eyebrows to ask for the inside story.

"You mean cases?"

"Sure." Shally shrugged.

"Yes. I presented Abram some information about one."

Shally whispered as if they were in a college dorm comparing titillating dating stories. "Tell me all about it."

Eliana clarified, "It was information he requested about a petition to review a freedom of speech case."

"I mean, how did he take it?" Shally smirked and shimmied her shoulders.

Julie frowned. "Don't you have work to do?"

"Just catching up on some girl talk. Not everyone is as married as you are. Miss Pearls here might be having more fun than you think."

"That's enough." Julie commanded.

Shally hopped off the desk and raised her right hand to her brow in a mock salute to Julie. Muttering expletives, she exited the office in a huff.

"I apologize for her attitude, Ana."

"I appreciate the rescue." Eliana sorted through the files on her desk.

Julie flipped through the pages of her planner. "You will find people around here become 'yes' men, to stay in the good graces with the powerhouses so they can secure favors from them. They think nothing of it. It's the new normal."

Ron opened the door and scanned each corner of the office.

Julie answered before he asked, "Shally just left. I don't know where Kirstie is."

Ron nodded and closed the door.

Julie explained, "You might want to stay in here on Thursdays and Fridays if you want to avoid the predators and actually get some work done."

"Both predators have hit on me already."

Julie lifted her left ring finger. "The wedding rings help me fend off the predators."

Eliana nodded. "I don't have a wedding ring, but 'Not tonight. I have to study for the bar' is working so far."

~~

After afternoon deliberations, Abram tossed a few files to Eliana. "See what you think about these."

Kirstie followed him into the office and smirked at Eliana as she closed the door.

Julie closed her eyes and sighed when the lock clicked.

Eliana stared at the closed door. *How can this be considered normal? How can Julie sit there and work as if nothing were going on behind those doors? How can she ignore this?*

Did Granddaddy know? If he did, why would he be friends with Abram? Why would he have wanted me to have this position around all this?

~~

Friday

Eliana secured her pearls around her neck, which had become part of her daily routine. *If Shally sees my pearls as a sign of righteousness, I'll wear them every day. Grandma, thank you for your example to me and your prayers. I'll need them.*

Fridays weren't casual in dress, but Friday lunch beverages apparently included more than soft drinks. Eliana poured her usual Dr.

Pepper, but Abram and Matt passed around their flasks and embellished their drinks. Eliana held her hand over the top of her cup.

Shally noticed. "Looks like Miss Pearls is going to pass on the good stuff."

"She's studying for the bar, you know." Ron added. "Can't drink from the bar 'til you pass the bar."

Matt put his arm around Eliana. "Hey, don't be too rough on my buddy here."

Eliana flushed at Matt's side embrace. *I hope no one gets the wrong idea.*

Abram took center stage and entertained the clerks with his vulgar stories. The climbers all howled in obedient laughter.

At least Abram's comments got them off my case.

It had been a long week, and the strain suddenly hit Eliana hard. She gulped down the rest of her Dr. Pepper and announced, "I'm going back to the office." But when she stood, her ankles wobbled.

Matt stood beside her and grabbed her around the waist. "You okay?"

Eliana leaned her hands on the table to gain her bearings. "Fine, thanks. Just tired."

"I'll walk up with you. You don't look so great."

Ron popped in, "I'll clear the table for you."

Matt answered, "Thanks." He secured one muscled arm around her ribs and guided Eliana out of the dining hall. "I don't think you should try the stairs. Let's grab an elevator."

Eliana's vision swirled and her legs went rubbery. "I think you are right." She had no choice but to lean on his strong frame. *Maybe I was wrong about Matt. I need these strong shoulders more than I thought.*

When they entered the elevator, Eliana shifted to lean against the wall and hoped she didn't slide to the floor. She held her hands over her face to try to somehow steady her spinning head.

Matt pressed 2, but as soon as the doors closed, he pressed STOP, grabbed her wrists, and slammed them against the wall of the elevator, locking her arms beside her head.

"No," Eliana slurred. *He put something in my drink.* "No. No. No. Le'me go. Shomeone will come. The alarm."

"Nope. No alarm on this one. It hasn't worked the whole time I've been here." Matt cocked his head and pressed against her wrists until she could no longer feel her fingers. He leaned in toward her face. "Now you and I can have some time alone. We can get acquainted right here, right now, just you and me. No one will come looking for us for a long time." He growled a sinister laugh.

"No. Lea'me alone. No." Eliana shook her head and tried to convince her muscles to muster enough strength to fight against his painful grip. None of them responded to her desperate plea. Her vision began to close in. Her legs grew weary and she drifted toward unconsciousness. *Whatever he added to my drink, it was more than alcohol.*

"Come on. Just relax. Have some fun."

"No. Shtop." Eliana's slurring words and helplessness infuriated her, and her heart drummed in rage. *God, I can't fight this. I need You to protect me. Dear Father God, help me.*

In spite of the drug, unusual strength surged in Eliana's limbs and brain. She jerked her arms down and away from Matt and slapped him hard across the face. "I said stop."

Stunned, Matt leaned back and rubbed his cheek. "All right already, feisty girl. We have plenty of time to get acquainted.

Meanwhile, I suggest you loosen up and learn to participate if you want to stick around. Otherwise, pack up, go home, and crochet doilies. You decide." He pressed the elevator button and stormed out as soon as the doors opened on the second floor.

Eliana took a few deep breaths and waited to put some distance between them before she exited the elevator. She leaned on the cool marble wall for a few seconds before she wobbled to the office.

"Are you sick?" Julie questioned when Eliana opened the door.

Eliana, still a little breathless, shook her head. "While Abram told his stories at lunch, Matt must have put some kind of drug in my drink. Then we got on the elevator, and he stopped it." She slid into her chair.

Julie pulled her chair near Eliana. "Typical. His father is—"

"Yeah, he told me. A political powerhouse."

"And if you report him, all guns will point at you, not him. Did he hurt you?" Julie lifted Eliana's chin to study her face.

"No. Just ..." Eliana shook her head and rebuked the tears that threatened to flood. She blinked hard to keep them at bay.

"Not a great 'welcome to D.C.,' is it?" Julie sighed.

"I'll be okay."

"Why don't you call it a day? I'll tell Abram you weren't feeling well and call you a cab."

"I don't want him to win." Eliana's chin quivered.

"He hasn't. You will recover, keep your dignity, and come back stronger next week. How about that cab?"

"If you are sure Abram won't mind.

"Believe me. A lot of convenient Friday afternoon sicknesses pop up around here."

"I'll take you up on it then. Thank you."

Chapter Three

As she entered her apartment, Eliana peered into the mirror above the key bowl at the reflection of her haggard face. She reached up and touched her pale cheeks. *God, what have I gotten myself into?*

Her eyes caught sight of the pearls in the reflection. They practically glistened and enticed Eliana's troubled heart to a place sparkling with peace.

Granddaddy told her he and her grandmother had an extravagant love, and they did. It carried them through the deaths of their first six children, three lost in miscarriages, then three sons who each died within weeks after birth.

That kind of suffering can ruin most marriages, but not theirs. Grandma had told her of those agonizing times. Each so full of hope, then those dreams buried—no, they were given back to God—with each child. But she always ended with her gratitude for the wonderful blessing of their seventh child, Grace, who became Eliana's mother. Named for the grace of God, which was sufficient for them.

Grandma, I need to see you.

~~

Saturday morning

During the night, the fog in her head had cleared. Eliana called her mom and packed up to go home.

"Mom?"

"I'm in the kitchen."

Eliana tossed her overnight bag by the door and headed toward the kitchen. "You can't imagine how good it is to be home."

Grace finished rinsing her hands in the sink and patted them dry before embracing her daughter. "Well, I can imagine how good it is to have you home. I've missed you so much." Grace welcomed her with the motherly hug she'd missed so much the past week.

"I see peaches."

"Yes. After you called, I went to the farmer's market and found some. Just finished slicing them to go over—"

"Pound cake?"

Grace nodded. "I couldn't help myself. It isn't every day my favorite daughter comes home to visit from Washington, D.C."

Eliana had forgotten how tired her mother looked these days. "How are you, Mom? Is everything settling down? The estate? The will?"

"I'm fine, sweetie. Everything is fine." Grace covered the peaches with plastic wrap and slid them into the refrigerator. "No glitches. Just going through the process. With your dad, I don't even remember doing these things. Guess I was in a fog, plus my dad helped. A lot."

"Is there anything I can do to help?"

Grace washed her hands, untied her apron, and put it away. "No. I'm muddling through. I've worked in a law office long enough to know how things work."

"Is the office closed out yet?"

"Actually, a group of attorneys have made a really good offer to buy the firm, so I'll have that plus the rental income. Dad left me some life insurance. That will help take care of my mom. Of course, the house is paid for ... Oh, and J.T.'s parents sent a letter and opened a checking account to help with final expenses. They'll maintain it for us for a few months until everything is settled."

Grace folded her arms in front of her. "Enough about all that. Tell me about your job. How was your week?"

"Well, I'm glad they at least did that. I haven't heard from the Barringtons in a long time."

"Hey, sis. How's the big D.C. lawyer?" Johnny squeezed her from behind like he hadn't seen her in years.

"Doing well, kiddo. Are you keeping Mom out of trouble?"

"Nah. She's hopeless." Johnny grinned when Grace pretended to swat at him.

"Well, are you staying out of trouble then?"

"You know me, sis. 'Trouble' is my middle name."

"Yeah, I know. Then, you turn on the charm, and we all just melt into a puddle."

Grace shook her head. "You two. How about some cake and fresh peaches?"

Eliana replied, "Perfect."

Johnny whined in a fake voice, "Mom, will you put some ice cream on mine, please?"

"Get your own ice cream, silly." Eliana poked him in the arm.

~~

Saturday afternoon

Grace thumbed through a magazine in her chair. From behind her, Eliana slipped both arms around her mom's neck and pressed her cheek against her mother's. "I need to go see Grandma."

Grace patted Eliana's arms. "I noticed you were wearing her pearls. She would love that, if she recognizes you. Keep in mind she hasn't recognized any of us in a long time. Don't be disappointed if you don't receive a response."

Eliana moved to the ottoman in front of Grace. "I know. I just need to talk to her."

"Think that's a great idea. Want me to come with you?"

"Actually, I need to talk to her alone."

"Is something wrong?"

"No. I just need to see her. I'm okay, promise. I'll take her some cake and peaches."

~~

The cheery paint of the locked-down unit always gave her hope that her grandma might be better. Wishful thinking.

Eliana entered Patricia's room. Grandma sat in her chair—hair clean but untidy—her open Bible cradled in her hands. Eliana pictured her back at home, reading from the pages of the precious Word of God she loved so much.

Those hands, gnarled now, had played the organ at church, worked hard to sew, garden, and preserve the harvest from their garden. They'd gathered eggs from the henhouse, churned whole milk from their cow, and tucked her two grandchildren under the quilts she'd made from salvaged shirts and dresses.

We were safe at her house. Safe, unrushed, and loved thoroughly and unconditionally. Grandma knew all about love. She read to us about it from her Bible and demonstrated it in her tender smiles, the meals she prepared, the way she spoke to Granddaddy, the kisses she lavished on us, and the powerful hymns she sang for us.

Patricia hadn't been able to decipher written words for years now. For a while, if someone quoted the beginning of a verse, she could finish it. She still held onto her Bible, her lifelong source of strength, comfort, and wisdom. Now, as much a part of her routine as dressing and eating, her Bible sat in her lap, where it belonged. *Perhaps she is reciting verses she memorized and is going over them with God in her head. I wish I knew.*

"Hi, Grandma. How are you today? It's Eliana."

When no response came, Eliana walked to her chair and placed the bowl of cake and peaches on one cushion of the sofa and sat on the other, beside her grandma. She reached one arm around her back and gave her a zig-zag scratch between her shoulder blades, like she used to ask her to do. Her fingertips reached through her lightweight dress to the bony shell that remained of her grandma. After many years of tireless work, plus the onset of dementia, her strength had been replaced with feebleness. Worst of all, her life of giving had changed to depending on others.

Eliana fingered through her grandma's white curls to comb them away from her eyes. "Your hair is so pretty."

Patricia's pale blue eyes stared at the wall in front of her. A picture of her with Milton and some other family pictures decorated the wall. *Could she see them? Did she remember the people and memories the photos captured?*

"Grandma, I love you so much. I miss Granddaddy. I miss talking with you both. Mom—your daughter, Grace—is okay. She's at home. We had pound cake with peaches today. I brought you some."

Eliana found a plastic spoon in a drawer, uncovered the bowl and spooned some of the peaches to her grandma's lips. She nudged her mouth with the spoon and Patricia opened her lips. The peaches slid into her mouth and she swished them around until she remembered to chew. When she managed to swallow them, she grunted.

"Isn't that good? Grace found some fresh peaches and cut them up. Aren't they juicy? This might be your pound cake recipe. What do you think?" She spooned a few more bites to her lips and watched them open again for more of the sweet deliciousness.

"Hi, Miss Patricia." A cheerful voice piped in. "Look, Miss Eliana's here to see you. How nice." She flitted around the room, checking for anything amiss.

"Hi, Mildred. How has she been?"

"Miss Eliana, she's just fine. She sits like this most days, in her own world just waitin' for the Good Lord to say it's her time. Of course, she holds the Good Book like it's a pot of gold, but that's what keeps her happy. If any of us tries to take it away, she gets real upset."

Mildred fluffed and tucked everything that needed fluffing and tucking. "Oh, Miss Patricia. That looks like some real good cake and peaches. Did Miss Eliana bring that for you? She must love you an awful lot to bring you something that delicious."

A smile crept across her grandma's face and her white curls bobbed.

"Looky there. I see that smile. You love her too, don't you Miss Patricia? You love her an awful lot, don't you?"

Patricia's cheeks rose as she squinted and smiled.

"Okay." Mildred patted Patricia on the shoulder. "I'll leave you two alone. Good to see you Miss Eliana. We're takin' real good care of your grandma. See you in a little while, Miss Patricia. We have a good dinner cookin' for you."

"Thank you, Mildred. I'm glad she still recognizes your voice."

"She's just fine, Eliana. Her and the Good Lord, they got everything all worked out, just fine."

After Mildred left, Eliana sighed. "Grandma, I hardly know where to start."

Does she even hear me? She moved a chair to sit in front of her grandma and leaned near her face. "Grandma, I need to talk to you. Can you hear me?"

Patricia's eyes shifted to focus on Eliana's eyes, then down to the pearls.

"Yes." Eliana's heart quickened at the recognition. "I'm wearing the pearls you gave me. You don't know how much it means to me to wear them. You taught me so much through the years about extravagant love, family, faithfulness, and God. I remember all of it. I remember you. I love you so much."

Her grandma's eyes shifted back to Eliana's and filled with tears.

"Grandma, if you can hear me, I need you to pray for me."

Patricia's head nodded and tilted to the side.

"I know Granddaddy wanted me to take the position with Justice Abram, but I don't know how long I can stay there. It's not what I expected at all. The justice is not what I expected. I had no idea what it would be like. They engage in so much sin, and no one is embarrassed. They all act like it's normal. Will you pray for me? I need to hear from God. I need to know what He wants me to do."

Patricia lifted the Bible.

"I know, Grandma. I read mine every day."

She pushed it to her.

Eliana took the Bible, opened to 1 Kings 16.

Patricia reached over and tapped the page.

"Okay. I'll read out loud for you. 'Ahab the son of Omri became king over Israel … he did evil in the sight of the LORD more than all who were before him. It came about, as though it had been a trivial thing for him to walk in the sins of Jereboam the son of Nebat, that he married Jezebel the daughter of Ethbal king of the Sidonans, and went to serve Baal and worshiped him. So, he erected an altar for Baal …'"

Eliana paused and looked at the words. *Evil. Trivial thing to walk in sin … God didn't want me to read to you. God wanted me to hear from Him.*

"This is exactly what I am dealing with, Grandma. I am working for a powerful man who does evil in the sight of the LORD. He and the people around him all do such evil, and no one thinks anything about it. They think it's trivial. Normal. What do I do?"

Eliana waited, hoping for some miraculous ability for her grandma to speak words of wisdom, but she stared at the wall in front of her. Eliana handed her Bible back to her. Patricia's moment of lucidity evaporated.

"I love you Grandma."

No response.

Eliana sang "Jesus Loves Me" while Patricia nodded in tempo.

"I need to get back, Grandma, but I want to pray with you for a minute before I leave."

After the prayer, Eliana kissed the wrinkled cheek of her beloved grandma, tossed the plastic spoon into the garbage, and gathered the empty bowl. "I love you. I'll be back to see you soon."

On her way out, she waved to Mildred, who was singing with a patient, encouraging them to clap with the music.

I wish I could hear her voice just one more time. I wish I could talk with Granddaddy. Thank you, Father, for giving me these wonderful leaders in my life. I know You used Grandma and her Bible to let me know You hear my plea. Please show me what You want me to do.

~~

"How was your trip? How did your grandma look? Everything okay?"

"She was sitting up and enjoyed the cake and peaches. She wasn't in distress or anything. Seemed to be fine. Mildred came in. She's so good with all the patients."

"Come sit at the table with me and have a cup of coffee. Tell me about it."

Eliana chose a vanilla latte coffee pod and pressed the button for the machine to heat the water. "I enjoyed the beautiful day. It was good to be out, clear my head, and see her. I asked her to pray for me. Think she heard me. How about you? How was your afternoon?"

After Eliana's cup filled, she tossed the empty pod in the trash and joined her mother at the table.

"I went through some papers. Nothing exciting. It just takes a while to close out things—"

"Mom, I can help you with anything you need me to do."

"Thanks, sweetie. I'm okay." She patted her open Bible. "I'm finishing up the Sunday School lesson for tomorrow. Exodus 8. God's people being distinct, or distinguished, from the ungodly. Two Hebrew words, *palah* and *peduwth* …"

Eliana lowered her head and tried to extinguish the tears that fired up and stung her eyes.

"Hey." Grace laid her hand on Eliana's arm. "What's going on? Talk to me. I'm your mom. I've known you longer than anyone, and I might be able to help."

"You always do, but you have enough to deal with." Eliana took a deep breath, lifted the mug, and blew on the steaming brew but put it back on the placemat to cool a little more. She glanced toward the open Bible.

"I want to be distinct, Mom. I want to be different from what I see at work, but I am already weary of the constant battle. Everywhere I turn …" *I'll spare her the sordid details.* "I asked Grandma to pray for me. I do think she heard me."

"She probably did. I'm pretty sure dementia patients can hear more than they can speak, so my guess is that she heard you and will pray for you. I imagine that's already part of her day." Grace smiled that beautiful, knowing smile that always brought a gift of extraordinary peace to its recipients.

"Hope she knew I was there. I don't want her to feel alone, but wish I could know for sure. I've always counted on her prayers, her wisdom. Like I did with Granddaddy and with you, too. It just feels like I am losing someone else whose prayers have helped me along the way. Of course, I know I can count on your prayers, and I'm not dismissing them at all. I just miss having a multitude of powerful prayer warriors. Every battle I faced was already prayed over by you all, and I miss that." Eliana swiped the hot tears from her cheeks.

"I miss them too." Grace slipped her arm around her daughter's shoulders. "I miss them and their prayers, but I am still here for you. I will always be available to lift you to the throne of God. Every single prayer is before His throne. Is there anything you want me to pray about, other than being distinct among your coworkers?"

"I just want to make sure I'm doing what God wants, not what I want."

"Are you still talking about this job or your career in general?"

"The job. I feel like I am the only Christian in an R-rated setting. No boundaries. No moral guideposts. No limits to what is acceptable to promote themselves or their agenda. And no shame about any of it."

"You aren't ignorant of the ways of the world. I'm confident you can handle yourself."

"I'm not being tempted. Don't get me wrong. I have no desire to be a part of that lifestyle. I just don't see how I can make a difference in a place that is so thoroughly entrenched in and blinded by corruption."

The look of concern on Grace's face melted again into her serene smile. "You remember about your name?"

"Yes. You've told me a hundred times." Eliana resisted rolling her eyes. She picked up her mug and sipped.

"When your dad and I prayed for a child and lost two with miscarriages, I prayed so fervently for Him to give us a child. He knew my desire to be a mom, but it seemed like God didn't answer me for a long time. Then, before I knew I was pregnant, He told me that we would have a child—you—and He would use you like he used Elijah, so people would know He is God. That's why I—"

Eliana nodded at the familiar phrases of the story. "—named me Eliana, the female form of the name Elijah. Yes. I love that story. Mom, did you ever talk with Grandma about that?"

"Of course, I did. I was thrilled, and so was she."

"Today, when I visited her, she handed me her Bible, open to 1 Kings 16—the part before Elijah speaks to the evil King Ahab. He is described as thinking it a trivial thing to walk in sins and he served Baal. That's exactly how I feel at work, Mom. I feel like I'm working among pure evil, and they see it as trivial."

Grace smiled. "Do you think that was a coincidence?"

"No. I don't, really. She had it open to that passage when I came in. Do you think it's possible she knew, or God told her something? I don't know what to think."

"I think God answered your prayer with His Word. Talk to Him and listen to Him. Look into the story that follows that passage. If you're to be used as Elijah—and God has already told me you are—I encourage you to be open to do what He tells you. I trust you, sweetheart, to do the right thing. But even more, I trust God to show you what to do."

Eliana nodded. "Thank you, Mom. I don't tell you often enough how much I love you."

"I love you too, sweetie."

"I'll let you return to your lesson. I'm going to my room to do some research."

~~

Eliana set her coffee on a coaster on her desk, booted up her computer, and searched for 'Baal.'

"A weather god, with particular power over lightening, wind, rain. Chief lieutenant of Lucifer. Associated with the bull, in strength and fertility, presides over the Order of the Fly, Lord of the flies. The Hebrew way of calling him a pile of dung."

Eliana chuckled. *That's fitting.*

In another article, "Ba'al ebub or Beelzebul claims to cause destruction through tyrants, to excite priests to lust, cause jealousies and murders, and bring on war. The priestess or female members, prostitutes, used sex to bring about a good harvest and the community perceived sexual unions as ways to influence the gods' actions towards them."

Well, something certainly turned up the lust dial where I work.

"Baal's followers sacrificed their children, often their firstborn, to gain personal prosperity."

Eliana sat up straight and read it again. *In the stack of files Abram just gave me, there was one about the right to life of a fetus and bringing charges against a doctor who performed a late-term abortion. Father God, is this what you are showing me? Do you want me to share with Abram about this? He didn't take my freedom of speech and sermons opinion very well. Show me what and how to represent You to Abram and to my co-workers.*

~~

Sunday morning

"Sleep well?" Grace scrambled eggs in a skillet. "You look like you feel better today. Eggs are almost ready. Put in some toast if you want."

"I did and I do, Mom, thanks." Eliana found a loaf of whole wheat, pulled out two pieces, set them in the toaster, and pressed the lever. "I took your advice, and I think I'm on the right track after all."

"Do I smell coffee?" Johnny rambled in, tugging his pajama bottoms up.

"Morning, Johnny."

Grace began, "Church begins in two hours,"

All three chorused in unison, "Manage your time wisely."

Eliana snickered. "Some things never change."

~~

The pastor began with a passage he quoted at her granddaddy's funeral a few weeks ago, 1 Corinthians 15. He spoke of the last trumpet and the dead being raised, everyone changing, and death being swallowed up in victory for the believers. All comforting words she had heard many times before, but her heart pricked at the last two verses in the chapter.

"But thanks be to God, who gives us the victory through our Lord Jesus Christ. Therefore, my beloved brethren, be steadfast, immovable, always abounding in the work of the Lord, knowing that in the Lord, your labor is not in vain."

Perfect! Eliana's heart soared. *My labor is not in vain. God put me there for a reason. He will give victory.*

Grace nudged Eliana, and they shared a smile, knowing those words written millennia ago were for Eliana at this specific day and hour.

After church, Eliana made a sandwich from leftovers, grabbed a can of Dr. Pepper, and headed out. "I'll eat on the road, so I can get back to D.C. I love you guys. See you soon."

Grace winked and blew a kiss as Eliana backed out of the driveway.

Lisa Worthey Smith

Chapter Four

Sunday night
Washington, D.C.

Eliana unpacked and washed a couple of loads of laundry in between searches online about the abortion issue Abram gave her. She gathered her thoughts for the argument for life and jotted down a few notes.

With no time to join the study group tonight, Eliana headed to bed. *Right now, I need a good night's sleep to face another week with this crowd more than I need the study time for the bar.*

Eliana set out her clothes for Monday, double-checked her alarm clock, and pulled her feet under the down comforter, secure in her mission for the week.

Thank you, Father, for filling my heart with renewed strength this weekend. Thank You for speaking through my grandma, my mom, and Your Word. I will do my best to remain steadfast and do what You want me to do.

With Your strength, I pray everything I do this week will honor You. Let me see everyone with Your heart, not with my fears or

expectations. I know my work for Your kingdom will not be in vain,
because You said it, and You are faithful to Your Word.
    Show me what You want me to do, moment by moment.
    In Jesus' name. Amen.

~~

Eliana had barely closed her eyes, when she 'woke up' in a dream, inside a palace in Samaria. King Ahab sat before her, strumming his fingertips on the arm rests of his massive throne.

As if he spoke them aloud, Eliana heard Ahab's thoughts. "I am King of Israel. My father, Omri, did well in purchasing this hill of Samaria. And I have done well in securing the Phoenician beauty beside me as my wife. With the alliance of her father, king of the coastal ports of Tyre and Sidon, I have expanded and enhanced my territory. Ahab, King of Israel. If only my father could see me now."

Could that be a little pride peeking out from under that crown?

Queen Jezebel, seated to his right, leaned over and lightly stroked her husband's arm. "My king." She fluttered her heavily outlined eyes toward Ahab and twirled her gemstone necklace with her right hand.

What a flirt. She's up to something.

"My queen, Jezebel." He pulled himself out of his thoughts of grandeur and glanced down. "Your father, Ethbaal, truly bestowed upon me a treasure when he gave me you to be my wife."

He's thoroughly entranced with her. No. He's seduced by her, and she is using all her ploys to reel him in.

Jezebel lowered her head with a demure smile. She nestled her hand within his on the arm of the throne. "And you, my king, my husband, are a great treasure to me."

Taking a moment for her adoring smile to fade, she bit her bottom lip, took a deep breath, and summoned tears she'd restrained from slipping down her cheek too soon.

Ahab squeezed her hand and leaned forward to look at her face. He cupped her chin and tilted her face to his. "Tell me. Are you unhappy?"

She shook her head and feigned a pout. "No."

"Do you wish for more jewels? More robes? I have already planned for you a palace in Jezreel, north of here. It might not be ivory lined as this one because I will use it as a military base. But you'll be safe and it will be cooler there for you. Tell me. What is it you desire? Why are these tears threatening to flow from your beautiful eyes? No tears must stain your exquisite face."

"My king." Her chin trembled.

Oh, she's good. That was a forced sob if I ever saw one. Is he really that gullible?

"Tell me now. I demand it." He tightened his grip on her hand. "Have I withheld anything from you? Ask. It will be done. Do not let me see you in this state."

Jezebel restrained her smile and kept her pout intact, held his gaze, and purred to him. "You know I was princess in my father's realm."

Ahab sat up straight and stomped one foot at the base of the throne. "And now you are queen."

"Yes, I am." She nodded, patted his hand, and tilted her head toward him to lock his gaze into hers. She drew her face closer to his and focused on his lips, inviting a kiss. Before his lips could reach hers, she began, "I am your queen and thankful to be by your side, my king. I want to serve you well—," Jezebel hesitated and smiled, "—in every respect."

This woman and her seduction tactics ... she will get anything she wants. Any-thing.

When he acknowledged the thinly veiled invitation with a nod, she raised one eyebrow and continued, "In my father's kingdom, I was also priestess to my gods. Please, my king, do not be dismayed with me."

"We have places of worship here." Ahab tried to reach her lips, but she pulled back just enough so that he could not.

"Yes, my king, for the old Israelite God. That was the old way. Now your people have a wonderful new king with new ideas and new ways." She hesitated. "And a new queen. Perhaps they could use some new gods."

Jezebel leaned in and tossed her hair to the back, offering him her neck, laden with his favorite perfume. "But you have no houses of worship for my gods. I was raised in service to Baal, the prince over all lightening, wind, rain—." She waited and looked up at him with a smile. "And fertility. Even my name, Jezebel, calls to him—'where is the prince?' I was a priestess to his consort, Lady Astarte, or in your language, Asherah, the goddess of fertility. I don't mind if some people worship the old god. But, how can I serve you fully and not call on my gods to protect us, to bring prosperity to this land? How can I seek Baal to bring the rain?"

She pulled herself close to his ear and whispered, "How can I beseech Astarte that she may fill my womb? I long to give you the children you deserve, my king, my husband, my lover. How can she hear me without a sacred pillar for proper worship?"

Ahab chortled and pulled her hand near his chest. "Let your tears be gone. You, my queen, shall have the best places of worship in the land. I will command it be done. Do not let those lovely eyes be reddened over that." Ahab lifted her slender hand to his lips and pressed a kiss to it. "It will be done, my queen."

Jezebel let her smile spread across her face and leaned over to reward the hand that held hers with a lingering kiss, closing her eyes in a passionate promise.

~~

Then, Eliana shifted to a scene outside in the heat with someone else. A rugged man, with a hairy mantle and leather belt. Elijah. He walked on the road to the capital of Israel, Samaria murmuring about how sickened he became at the asherahims Ahab had built and the evil that occurred within them. The sacrifices they willingly offered of their firstborn infants to Baal, instead of dedicating them to the LORD made his heart physically ache, and Eliana vicariously felt it in her own.

Elijah passed by gleaming temples with enormous numbers of earthen jars waiting to hold the dead babies slaughtered to these false gods, the prostitutes waiting for "worshippers" to enter, the willing participants chatting while they waited their turn to enter the evil house.

Eliana felt her own blood rush to her neck and pulse with fury as she watched Elijah's do the same.

He called out, "Oh, my people. Why have you turned your hearts from YHWH and defiled the land with such evil ashtereeth poles, altars, and temples? How can you be so blind? Do you not remember Adonai, our LORD our God is one? *Shema Israel. Shema Israel YHWH, Elohim, YHWH echad ...*"

The Shema. This is what the Jews were to remember when they walked, when they lay down. It was to be on their hands, on their foreheads, and on their door posts.

"You shall fear the LORD your God; you shall serve Him ... you shall not go after other gods, the gods of the peoples who are round about you."

Elijah powered his way through the rowdy Samarian crowd to reach the king's residence. "Move aside. Let me pass by here."

Some snickered and pointed at Elijah. A young man came to Elijah, pulled on his cloak, and jeered, "Look, a dusty camel comes into town wearing this hairy saddle! Tell me, sir, are you a camel? Have you lost your rider?"

Several of the young men snickered and gathered around to join in. One tugged at his leather belt and cried out, "Here is his rein. Let's lead this lost beast to the stables."

Elijah jerked his mantle back, elbowed away the man who pulled at his belt, and firmed his stance. "Stand aside. I am here to see the king. Be out of my way."

The laughter swelled among the crowd. "This crazy man wants to see the king? Perhaps Ahab wants to ride this camel to Jezreel to visit his queen."

Elijah prayed with every step through the antagonistic swarm. "YHWH, give me strength to do this. I need Your hand upon me now."

No one hindered his progress after he spoke those words.

When he reached the keepers of Ahab's court, he spoke to the guards, "I am here to see the king of Israel, Ahab."

The guards sneered at each other and then eyed Elijah from head to toe. One pushed the tip of his sword into Elijah's mantle, lifted his eyebrows and asked, "Who are you? Why do you think the king wants to see you?"

"I am Elijah, from Tishbe. I am here to speak to the king. He will see me. Announce me at once."

One guard told a servant behind the gate to deliver the message while the other kept the tip of his sword inches away from Elijah's heart.

From behind the wall, someone announced his request, and Ahab replied, "I am bored. Send him in."

Two muscular guards grabbed Elijah's arms and jerked him into motion. "Filthy." One guard snarled at Elijah.

Brutes.

The other echoed with a smirk, "Want to take a bet on how long the king will tolerate this hairy intruder? Will you take his head, or shall I?"

His escorts shoved Elijah toward the gold and ivory throne.

Eliana's blood ran cold, and she imagined Elijah's did even more. The things going on outside this palace, and Ahab just sat there. How could the king of ten tribes allow such evil, such shame, on Israel? The guards call Elijah filthy, yet they serve this man who brings evil pagan gods, Baal and Astarte, into the house of Israel.

Elijah inhaled a long breath.

Eliana felt him pray,

"Blessed be the LORD Almighty, the one God of all, who gives me strength. Whom shall I fear? Certainly not this godless man."

Elijah stiffened his shoulders, straightened his mantle, and spoke with authority, "King Ahab, I have come to let you know YHWH has been patient with your idol worship. But you must realize this turning away from Almighty God will bring judgment."

Ahab threw up his hand to dismiss the idea. "Didn't Moses already warn us in the Torah that the rain would cease and the land would not give forth its produce if we should worship other gods? Yet, nothing happened as yet."

Elijah nodded. "Only because of His lovingkindness and mercy. You don't even recognize that. Now you will see that not merely shall Moses' words, but mine also will be fulfilled. As surely as the LORD, the God of Israel lives." He paused to restrain his emotions and lift his shoulders. "—before whom I stand, there will be neither dew nor rain these years, except by my word." The words echoed through the halls of the palace.

The guards reached out to terminate this insulter of the king, but Elijah jerked his arms away from them and strode out of the room, unhindered.

By the time Ahab shouted, "Be gone!" Elijah had already set his feet on the street again.

The townspeople gathered to continue their taunts. "Tell us about your important meeting with the king. It didn't last long."

The young men gathered around him and continued their harassment. "Tell us, did he see your finery and request a ride to the next town? Or, did he appoint you to his court? No? Did he offer you a fine robe to replace this thing or perhaps a nose ring to bring you into his stable? Go back to the desert, you camel."

The mob slapped at his mantle and shoved him along the path. Mothers pulled their children near to protect them from the hostile throng.

Eliana's heart hammered. She jerked in her bed to avoid the clashes and wrestled with her pillow.

The taunts escalated. Elijah's palms sweat, and his lungs couldn't get enough air, *YHWH! Where are You? Don't let me die at the hand of this mob that Ahab's gods will be glorified!*

God, help him, she prayed.

Their jeers faded into the background of Elijah's hearing. As though invisible walls divided them into two groups, the crowd separated. Elijah passed among them with no one able to touch him.

The LORD spoke to him as he walked in the midst of the people, supernaturally restraining them from harming him. "Go away from here and turn eastward, and hide yourself by the brook Cherith, which is east of the Jordan. There, you will drink of the brook, and I have commanded the ravens to provide for you there."

"Yes, LORD. I will do as You have said. I beg You, let my people see that you alone are God Almighty."

Eliana bolted up in bed, fully awake, her heart clamoring up her throat. She surveyed her surroundings.

My room.

My bed.

It was just a dream. Probably because of what I read in 1 Kings.

Deep breath.

Just a dream. Go back to sleep.

Eliana laid her head on her pillow, but replayed the dream in her head. *You told Mom You would use me like You did Elijah. God, give me strength and courage to remain steadfast and follow Your direction.*

Chapter Five

Monday morning

Markham exited Abram's office and glanced toward Eliana. For the first time, she approached Eliana's desk, jutted out one hip and rested her hand on her waist. "Dear Elly Ann, I heard you had an opinion to share about the pastor's coercion tactics from the pulpit. Rest assured, Abram hears all points of view. He told me about your little talk. It was really cute. Don't be discouraged. You will learn though. You'll learn."

"*Eliana*. My name is Eliana."

Markham turned from her and made a point to apply her lipstick in the mirror before she went out. She tucked in her shirt with a nod toward her. "Eliana, dear, you just need to remember who is in charge and provide what they want. That's how you get ahead. You won't get anywhere by yourself. And believe me, you don't want to be left out in the cold, or be on the wrong side."

Eliana fumed. Before she could comment, the Louboutin heels clicked the hall floor toward the next victim. *How could this be? How could Granddaddy have been friends with such a man?*

The clerks filed in, Ron and Shally first, then Matt. No one glanced at Eliana.

Julie flew in out of breath and tossed her things behind her desk. "Sorry. I'm running a little later than usual."

"Everything okay?"

"Yeah. Fine. Thanks. How about you?" Julie laid out her planner and checked the appointments.

"I went home for the weekend and that really helped."

"Good. Glad to hear it. This is not an easy job. You're doing great. The clerks in with Abram?"

"I don't know about Kirstie. Markham came out, then Ron, Shally, and Matt went in."

When Julie buzzed in to let Abram know the time, the three clerks came out of the office, followed by Abram.

"Send Kirstie a get-well card from the office," Abram commanded with no further explanation.

~~

At lunch, Shally nudged Eliana. "I guess you heard by now that Kirstie had another abortion. No one is taking credit, but I have my suspicions."

"No. I didn't. I'm sorry to hear that. That's so sad."

"Are you kidding? It's not sad for her. She has her whole life to get married and have kids. Why should she put aside her career and everything she's worked for? Small inconvenience to curry Abram's blessing and referrals that will usher her into the lifestyle and career of her dreams."

Ron joined in. "You talking about Catwalk Kirstie? Anyone 'fess up to this one yet?"

Matt sat down. "It wasn't me this time. Promise. I already paid out enough money on that girl."

Shally caught their attention and answered Ron's question with a tilt of her head toward Abram. Ron and Matt smiled at Shally, nodded, and gave a thumbs-up.

"Way to go, Kirstie," Ron whispered.

"Way to go, Abram." Matt laughed.

Abram started his comments on the arguments of the morning cases and gradually got around to the females who attended, how they were dressed, and his regular vulgar insinuations. The groupies hung on every word and practically cheered him on.

Eliana sipped on her Dr. Pepper. *It really is like Elijah's time. Sacrificing babies is a trivial thing to these people. They don't feel any guilt or shame over it. No remorse. No acknowledgement of the value of life, much less God or His laws. They don't seem to know God at all.*

~~

When Julie and Eliana were alone, Eliana brought up Kirstie. "I can't say I was shocked, but it is so sad to think of …"

"It probably happens more than you think."

"I know in college and even in law school, a few girls had abortions. They said they weren't ready to start a family … wanted to have their career first and all that. The girls didn't want to interrupt their career to be a single parent, and either they didn't want to marry the father or the father didn't want to marry them. I have a friend who is adopted. I always thought that was a better option."

Julie stopped typing on her computer and frowned at Eliana. "There are a lot of circumstances you might not think about, though. What if you were married and already had a child with special needs and got pregnant, even though you used birth control? What if that pregnancy would likely cost you your job, and your husband's job didn't include insurance or enough income to support the family?"

"Julie?" The blood drained from Eliana's face.

Julie nodded. "What else could I do?"

"They can't fire you for taking maternity leave."

"They wouldn't have to fire me. I'm on a one-year contract through an agency, like you and the clerks. They just don't renew that contract if someone is out very long. It's too easy to replace us. Most people use these positions as a temporary stepping stone to build their resume and establish contacts."

"I'm so sorry. I had no idea."

"Thanks." Julie's eyes drifted to the ceiling. "I think of that child often. He, or she, would be eight by now. We wanted to have several children, but we also knew our situation would not allow it. We thought it would be better this way."

Eliana had no words for Julie's shattered dreams and aching heart.

Julie shrugged and focused again on her computer. "There is a little clinic near here. When they are too late for the Plan B pill, I refer them there. Very professional, clean and discreet. They have a back entrance if we call Markham and set it up."

"Markham, that woman who comes to see Abram?"

Julie nodded. "The foundation she works for is privately funded and lobbies for free abortions on request. In Kirstie's case, they will pay the bill for her procedure, because Abram requested it.

"Most of the people who work here are very career-driven. They've invested a lot of time and money in their educations, and they expect to score powerful jobs and make a high income. Rather than spend the time working their way up the ladder, they take shortcuts that will assure them quick results. Those who do tend to get quick promotions, recommendations, and frankly, influential high-paying positions. It's the way it works around here. Especially with Abram. The other justices, not so much. Abram has already sent a letter of recommendation for Kirstie to obtain a position with a law firm whose clients are billionaires."

Julie's cell phone rang, and her eyebrows furrowed when she answered. "What did the doctor say? Are you going to be able to pick up her medicine? Okay. Good. Thank you. See you after work."

"Emma sick?"

"Yes. That's why I was late this morning, trying to make her comfortable. Todd took her to the doctor and is picking up her prescription now. She'll be fine."

"Good. I'm thankful for that."

"We've been pretty lucky. She's been in the hospital a couple of times, but nothing lately."

"Mind if I put her on my prayer list?"

"If you believe in that stuff, that's fine. I don't mind. Did you sign the card for Kirstie yet? I need to take it to the mailroom." Julie handed her the card.

Eliana wrote, 'Kirstie, you are in my prayers. Eliana' and put the card in the envelope. "You already have it addressed, so I'll take it down to the mailroom, if you want me to."

"Sure. That would be good. Thanks."

Eliana pulled out her cellphone as she strode down the hall. "Hey, Johnny. Is Mom there?"

"Nope. Gone to get groceries."

"Will you leave her a note for me?"

"Sure."

"Ask her to add a couple of people to her prayer list for me. A special-needs girl, Emma, who is sick, and a girl from work."

"Gonna' tell me her name or you want me to guess?"

"No. But she just had an abortion, and I wanted to cover her in prayer."

"Did she have a complication with it or something?"

"No. Not that I know of."

"So, what do I tell her to pray about? Everyone I know who's had an abortion did fine."

"Johnny, you're in high school. How many people do you know who have had abortions?"

"I'm a senior, in case you forgot. And I know plenty. Bella had one last year. No problem."

"Your girlfriend?"

"Yeah. I think her pills were off or we messed up with her dates or something. Anyway, a lot of our friends have had them too. Where have you been? Hiding under a book? It's a pretty simple deal. In and out quick and it's done. No big deal. Not like having a heart transplant or something."

"Johnny, will you please just pass along the message?"

"Sure thing."

Shally and Ron came toward her in the hallway.

Shally asked, "On a mission?"

"Taking this card for Kirstie to the mailroom."

"Oh. Big mission. That should earn you huge points with Abram. I can tell you what he really likes, if you want."

Ron put his arm around Shally's waist and gave her a squeeze. "Good old Shally, always ready to shell out."

"Well, a girl has to do what a girl has to do." Shally winked. "I have my eye on a certain firm, and Abram has the connections to get me in with them. We have a few more meetings coming up—," she fluttered her eyelashes, "—to go over all the options."

Eliana ignored both of them.

"What's wrong with you?" Ron blocked her way. "Are you that much of a prude? Or just holier than thou? You really want to be a secretary all your life? A nice-looking girl like You? Ditch the buttoned-up grandmother clothes and dress like you're here to do business. You can hook up with your choice of lawyers and have it made. I'm not one to hold grudges. I can set you up and you'll be off to a big-time firm."

"Not interested, Ron. We've already been through this." Eliana tried to side step him.

Ron stepped to the side to block her path. "We heard you left Matt in the lurch. Big mistake, Miss Purity in Pearls. He was not happy about that. If you ever want to practice law, I suggest you make it up to him pretty soon."

Eliana frowned. "Move, please. I have work to do, and I suggest you both get to work too."

Shally saluted. "Oh, yes ma'am. We have work to do. We'll get the job done." She released her salute and added, "I don't promise any folders or computer work though."

Eliana shook her head, left them giggling in the hall, delivered the card to the basement mailroom, then headed to the fourth-floor library to gather more information for Abram.

The statistics on abortion and the jars by the temples in her dream mingled together into a horrid picture. All those empty jars, ready to hold children, even back then. I never dreamed someone like Julie would have had an abortion. I never dreamed Johnny would agree to that.

Dear Lord, what am I to do? I'm supposed to present my research to Abram Thursday. What will I say? How will he react?

~~

Tuesday

On his way to court, Abram handed Eliana more case files petitioning for review. "Work on the top four issues first. Have me some background information by Thursday."

"Instead of the abortion case or along with it?"

"Save that one for later. Work on these for now."

"Yes, sir."

Eliana thumbed through the stack from top to bottom. First case - Purge schools and all government agencies from "offensive" holidays, Easter and Christmas, because Christianity must not be favored above any other religion.

Second case – Inclusion of Muslim prayers, prayer mats, the Qur'an and other literature in all public classrooms. Install statues of Buddha in the halls of public buildings, including schools, with incense burning to protect the occupants and instill peace, so all students will be included.

Third case – Criminalize hate crimes including statues, pictures, books, and online remarks about historical battles and leaders. Remove all references to the holocaust in school books and online.

Fourth case – Shift the burden of proof to police officers who detain, restrain, or fire a weapon on a criminal or suspected criminal, so they must prove they were in imminent danger of death or bodily harm, or someone else's.

Fifth case - Allow and encourage non-citizens to vote, to diversify and equalize the masses.

Sixth case – Allow communities to establish Sharia' law.

How could this country have come so far away from God? Before the Supreme Court of the United States are rulings to further purge any Christian influence. No wonder we are in such turmoil. Some courts have already seen suits to remove "In God we trust" and "under God" from the pledge of allegiance. How long, Lord, will You tolerate this? How long before you allow us to crumble from within?

Eliana straightened the files by tapping them on her desktop. "Julie, if you don't need me for anything, I think I'll go work in the library this morning. Think that will be okay?"

"That's fine. Everything is under control here. Go ahead. Sounds like you have a lot of research to do."

Eliana nodded, folded her laptop, and lowered it along with the files into a satchel. She slung it over her shoulder and patted her pocket to make sure her phone was there, then headed to the third floor.

Great. Matt is coming toward me. I'm not going to hide from him. She held her head high and looked him in the eye. "Good morning."

"Morning. Where you off to now?"

"Research."

"I guess that means the library."

"It's quiet there. I can get a lot done."

Eliana continued toward the spiral staircases. *No elevator rides with this guy.*

Matt stopped. "You know, I just remembered. I have some research to do too. Maybe I'll see you there later."

Eliana headed up the steps without replying. Her stomach churned. *I shouldn't have told him I was going to the library. At least Olivia, should be on duty. I'll have someone there, if I need them.*

~~

Deep into her study, Eliana read that Islam is more than a religion and covers every aspect of Muslim's social, cultural, religious, military, and political lives. They consider only their obligation Sharia' law, because Islamic laws supersede any other laws. Eliana read article after article about the Qur'an and its mandates. She was appalled to learn that Muslims have a permanent command to hate Jews and Christians and not take them as friends. Sacred Hadith, Bukhari, vol 4, book 55, number 657 read "The Muslim prophet Jesus will return to earth with Muhammad and will cast all Christians to hell, and kill all Jews, in order that Muslims may go to Paradise."

More than a little unnerving to see practicing Muslims with that mission in government positions.

"Sura 9: Jihad (warfare against non-Muslims) is a permanent obligation on the Muslim community until the entire world made the Dar al Islam. With three options for the 'People of the Book' (those who had a holy book prior to Muhammad): 1. They may convert to Islam. 2. They may be killed. 3. They may pay the jizya (non-Muslim tax) and be subjugated to Islamic law having little rights as non-Muslims under the law. Pagans and others who had no holy book prior to Muhammad must either convert to Islam or be killed."

Permanent obligation to jihad against non-believers. Eliana noted that phrase and others, for reference for her meeting with Abram.

"Fight the unbeliever wherever you find them and lie in wait for them in every stratagem of war ... fight the people until they testify that there is no deity worthy of worship except Allah."

Islamic Law specifically allows, and in some cases obliges, Muslims to lie to non-Muslims if doing so furthers the cause of Islam. "When a person who has reached puberty and is sane voluntarily apostatizes from Islam, he deserves to be killed. In such a case it is obligatory for the caliph (or his representative) to ask him to repent and return to Islam. If he does, it is accepted from him, but if he refuses, he is immediately killed ... there is not indemnity for killing an apostate since it is killing someone who deserves to die."

Under Islam, 'boys for play" is not only allowed, it is widespread. Men can purchase boys as young as eleven for sexual slavery. Owning boys is considered a status symbol. One man boasted of having three thousand boys over a twenty-year period, even though he was married.

Widespread. Revolting.

Eliana scanned another article about child brides, noting over a fourth of Muslim girls in the Middle East are married before they are fifteen. They indulge it as "an old tribal custom based on Muhammad's marriage to Aisha, who was about nine years old, while rejecting other documents that suggest Aisha was about nineteen.

Another article told of Islamic female circumcision, "to keep them in line, pure, and healthy." Girls are held down and teachers and midwives used scissors …

Eliana flinched and gasped out loud when she felt a strong hand clamp onto her thigh.

Matt had slipped into the chair next to her.

"What are you doing?" She tried to remove his hand, but he pressed it harder on her leg.

He put on a charming, smooth voice. "Let's not make a scene. I'm not going to hurt you. I just wanted to give you another chance. We can play nice or we can play rough and dirty. It's up to you."

She dug her nails into his hand, but he only tightened his grip on her leg. "I'm not interested in either. Get your hand off me and leave." Eliana looked past Matt for the librarian who was not at her desk.

Matt smiled and shook his head. "Olivia's not there. She's taking a break."

"If you don't leave, I'll break something of yours." Eliana reached up with her free hand to slap his face.

Matt grabbed her hand in mid-swing and mouthed a kiss to her.

"Go away. I am not interested. Final warning. If you don't leave me alone, I'll report you."

He lifted his eyebrows, shook his head, and spoke slow deliberate threats. "No, Miss Purity in Pearls. You won't do that because this is your final invitation. I'd rather invite you than warn you, but you can be sure there is a warning here. You have no idea how good I can make your life, or how painful I can make it."

"Get out. Now." She enunciated between clamped teeth.

"Your choice."

The way Matt's eyes roamed over her infuriated Eliana. He pressed his grip harder, pinching her leg to her bone. The pain took her breath and brought an unintended gasp. *I will not let him see me cry. I will not.*

Matt shrugged. "Too bad. Could have been fun."

"Get out." Eliana seethed from her clenched jaw.

Matt slowly unclamped his hand and stood to leave.

Eliana resisted bashing his head with her laptop. *What a jerk*. She jumped at the sudden buzz in her pocket and pulled out her phone. "Mom." Eliana took a good breath and commanded her voice not show any emotion before she swiped to answer it. "Hi, Mom. What's going on?"

"Hi, sweetie. I received your message and had you on my mind. Just wanted you to know I've been honoring your prayer requests. Update me when you have time. I don't want to bother you at work. Everything else okay?"

Eliana rubbed her aching leg. "Thank you. Yes, everything's fine. Love you. We'll talk soon, bye."

~~

Ron, Matt, and Shally stopped talking when Eliana drew up her chair to the lunch table. Their snickers gave evidence that her encounter with Matt in the library had made it to the gossip mill.

I wonder if his version of the events remotely resembles the truth.

Thankfully, Abram took center stage and held court, so his groupies had no opportunity to ridicule her. Julie sat attentive and professional.

Eliana waited for the others to leave the table first, so she could walk alone. *I'm not making any difference here, Lord. I am surrounded by people who are totally immersed in themselves and mock me for living according to Your laws. Show me, Father. Show me what to do.*

~~

Thursday

Abram opened the door and asked Eliana to come in. "Close the door behind you."

Eliana balanced the stack of case files on her left arm and used the right to close the door behind her.

"Sit." Abram motioned to the leather chair beside his desk.

Eliana pulled at her pearls, making sure they were in place, and asked God to guide her words. She stretched her arms forward to keep the files in her lap from falling.

Abram rolled his chair to Eliana's side of the desk. "So. What do you have on those six issues?"

He listened without comment while she reviewed the background information she'd found on Islam and Buddhism. Then he nodded and motioned his hand in a circle, as if to fast-forward.

Eliana spoke of the removal of Christian elements in the schools and other public places. "Your honor, if we remove Christ, and replace Him with these others religions, we are doomed."

"So, you think we should replace our republic with a theocracy, and one lone god to rule us?"

"Your honor, I'm sure you know more than I about the foundations of this republic and the founding fathers who—"

"Never mind. I've heard that one before. Let's talk about your behavior here."

"Sir?" Eliana's neck warmed.

He reached back to a file on his desk and opened it. "I'm rather surprised, I must say. I didn't expect this from Milton's granddaughter." He lifted a paper and scanned it. "Tell me about Matt."

"Sir? What about him?"

"Human resources gave me this sexual harassment report against you. Matt says you have groped and accosted him twice in this building. Once in an elevator and again in the library. When he refused your advances, you slapped his face and scratched his hand. Here's a picture." He handed a photo of a scratched hand to Eliana.

"Sir, no. That's not what happened at all. He—"

"You didn't slap him or scratch his hand?"

"I did, your honor, but—"

"Eliana. You are here because your grandfather wanted you to have a great start to your legal career. If you have this kind of hostile workplace environment and sexual harassment report on your record, how far do you think you will go?"

Eliana shook her head. *What is happening here? How can Matt get away with this?*

Abram leaned toward her and took on a fatherly demeanor. "I understand how certain favors are used for career advancement. Lobbyists often visit me to persuade me to lean toward certain rulings. Everyone does it. I understand that. However, if you are looking to advance your career, and I hope you are, I suggest you go about it with a more willing partner. Matt has the connections to bury you."

His eyes burrowed into her, making her skin crawl.

Abram leaned back in his chair. "Having said that, I want you to know that Matt came to me to let me know about this situation." He hesitated and pursed his lips.

He is waiting for a reaction from me. He wants to see if I will be willing to beg him …

Abram strummed his fingers on the papers. "Matt has a magnanimous spirit and is willing to be generous to you. He agreed, as a favor to me, to withdraw the complaint, if you agree to leave him alone. Now, that's not too much to ask, is it? It is more than fair."

"I ... Sir, I don't know what to say. It wasn't that way—"

Abram shook his head and lifted his hands to dismiss the rest of her thought. "I honestly don't care. What you do is your business, but as a long-time friend to your grandfather, I wanted to give you the opportunity to make this stain on your employment record go away, so you don't throw away your entire legal career."

"Justice Abram, I want to keep my job."

"All right then. Learn to follow the rules. Go." He motioned toward the door. As Eliana stood, he tore up the paper with a flourish and followed her out. Abram went on to his next meeting, Eliana to her desk.

Brilliant. If I file a counter complaint against Matt, he will cry retaliation. He won before I ever had a chance to file a complaint. If I had photographed the bruises on my leg ... "He said/she said" usually works in favor of the first plaintiff. Eliana set the files on her desk, stood over them, and stared at nothing in particular.

Julie looked at her. "You okay?"

"Blindsided, that's all. New job, new rules. Rules I didn't expect from this level. Junior high, maybe. Honestly, Julie, I've never been around so many adults who have so few scruples. For some reason, my back must have a bullseye target plastered on it."

"It's definitely 'sink or swim' around here sometimes."

"I'm still afloat, but I've got to learn how to identify the sharks."

Julie chortled. "Just open your eyes and look around. They are always circling."

Eliana nodded. "Isn't that the truth?"

"You know I see almost everything that comes to his desk. I saw the complaint Matt filed."

"Great. So, you saw what he accused me of. Unbelievable. I have to say you warned me about him."

"His teeth are sharp and always looking for new blood. I'm sorry he tried to take a bite out of you. What are you going to do?"

"Abram said Matt made a magnanimous offer to 'make it go away' if I agreed to follow the rules. I told him I wanted to keep my job. Abram tore it up."

Julie folded her arms and leaned on her desk. "That's just his copy. The original is in HR."

"Well, it gave Abram an opportunity to flaunt his power to me. He probably thinks I'm intimidated by that, even ingratiated to him, maybe even to Matt. I do need this job, and I want my career to stand for something, make a difference, for good."

Julie sighed. "Oh, the ideals of youth."

"Really, Julie. I'm a Christian and I am not ashamed of it. All my life I wanted to use the law to point people to Christ, to let them see true justice, mercy, forgiveness, grace—"

"Admirable, but I'm afraid the same sharks will circle you if you use that theory here. Some of the justices lean toward the ten commandments and that sort of thing, but Abram has something he holds over them. They argue one way, but in the end, most of them follow Abram. In his mind, the end justifies the means, and he is king over all."

"King Ahab won't rule long like that."

"Who is Ahab?"

"I meant Abram. Sorry, I studied a little about King Ahab over the weekend."

"A foreign case?"

"King Ahab in the Bible. Actually, my name, Eliana, is the feminine version of the name Elijah. He was the prophet who warned Ahab about disobeying God. God used Elijah to demonstrate His power to many people, so they would know He is God."

Julie's phone rang and she grabbed it. "Yes. Good. What did the doctor say? Can't he prescribe something else? A generic? I know. I don't expect you to … Todd?" She looked at the phone for a reply that didn't come.

Eliana asked, "How's Emma doing? Is she any better yet?"

Shally and Ron opened the door. "Is he gone to conference yet?" Julie nodded.

Shally came in and handed Julie an envelope. "Will you leave this on his desk and ask him to open it before he leaves for the day? It is an invitation to a special-called meeting he'll be very interested in."

Julie picked up a sticky note and wrote "Open before you leave, from Shalom." She stuck it to the front of the envelope and took it into Abram's office.

Shally waited until Julie was inside the office, before she leaned over Eliana's desk with a smirk on her face. "You really shouldn't have been so mean to Matt, you bad girl. No telling what your punishment's going to be."

Before Eliana could respond, Shally and Ron ducked out the door and Julie returned to her desk.

Childish behavior. They think everything is a game, and I'm their pawn. Granddaddy would say to take the high road, turn the other cheek, give them enough rope and they'll hang themselves. Mom would agree with turning the other cheek. God, help me to put aside my anger and see them through Your eyes. I need You to show me— Eliana picked up her vibrating phone.

"Hi, Mom."

"Eliana. I'm so sorry to bother you at work. I had a call this week from the group who was going to buy out the practice. They said that they're no longer interested, and I would receive a letter about it. The letter came today that confirmed they pulled out of the deal, and with it was a small note on a separate piece of paper that says, 'If you have any questions, just ask your daughter.' What's going on? What do they mean?"

Matt. He found out and sabotaged the deal. "I don't know, Mom. I'll see what I can find out."

"Honey, we need this to go through. If I did something wrong, why didn't you come to me?"

"No, Mom. You did nothing wrong. I didn't do anything either to stop the deal, but I'll see what I can find out and let you know. I'm sorry. I love you."

"But the note says you do know why. I don't understand." Grace sobbed.

"Mom, please don't cry. I don't know what happened, well, I might know, but I will have to do some checking. Try not to worry. I need to go. I love you. We'll figure it out. I promise."

Eliana hung up the phone and turned to Julie. "Do you happen to know Matt's sister? He said she's in corporate law here in D.C."

"No, I don't know her or anything about her except what Matt has said about how powerful she and the rest of his family all are."

"I'm going to find Matt."

"You'd better have on your fighting gloves."

"That shark may have teeth, but he doesn't have weapons that compare to mine."

Matt and Kirstie stood in the hallway, just outside the clerks' offices. Kirstie leaned against the wall with her hands behind her and Matt faced her, one hand propped on the wall behind her. "Matt, I need to talk with you," Eliana said.

The twosome turned their heads toward Eliana. Matt spoke quietly to Kirstie while Eliana approached them.

Kirstie giggled and Matt pressed away from the wall and addressed Eliana. "Yes, ma'am. I am at your service."

"Tell me what you did."

He took an imposing military pose with his hands on his hips. "Who me? I don't know. You tell me. What did I do?"

"I know about the HR report."

"Yeah, well, you naughty girl. I hope you've learned your lesson. Sexual harassment isn't becoming of you Miss Purity in Pearls." He wagged a finger toward Eliana. "I have a feeling your potential employers wouldn't hire someone who creates such a hostile workplace environment. Maybe, if you'll play nice, we can still work something out."

Kirstie covered her smile.

"Tell me about the attorneys who wanted to buy out my grandfather's practice."

"Yeah. I heard about that. Small world, huh? Too bad they no longer want to buy into it. They offered considerably more for Moore and Barrington than most small-town practices are worth. Wish it could have worked out differently for you and your mom. Heard she needs the income, after Milton's heart attack and all that."

"You did more than hear about it; you orchestrated it."

"Now, you give me too much credit. Why would I do such a thing?"

"Oh, you don't have the power, but you could have blackmailed someone, the way you're trying to manipulate me."

"Such a nasty accusation. I much prefer the word 'power.' You see, as I told you before, I do have that kind of power. The power to influence people. If you had me on your side, I might use some of that influence to turn that deal around, but as it is, I just used up all my generosity forgiving you for all those unwanted attacks against me."

"We both know the truth," she hissed through gritted teeth.

He shivered with a flair. "The truth is I feel so violated. It will take me a long time to recover. I hope I don't have to sue for pain and suffering, punitive damages. No, Miss Purity in Pearls, I just don't feel inclined to turn around any deals today."

God, help me. What do I say? What do I do?

"You think you have power. And I see what you're doing, what you've already done. Just so you know, I don't fear your kind of power."

Matt pretended to tremble in fear again. "You going to pull out a magic cape and show us your superpowers?"

Kirstie snorted and looked both ways down the hall before she spoke, "I'd like to see that."

Eliana began, "I don't have to have a cape—"

"No, Kirstie, her power is in her pearls." Matt pointed to Eliana's necklace. "They are glowing. We'd better take cover."

"I am not threatened by you. God will protect me. He said no evil will befall me. He gives angels charge concerning me, to guard me."

"Well, there you go." He tossed up his hands. "I'm sure I'm no match for an angel. When do you expect him to jump in and protect you? I'll go get my light sabre."

"You may not understand it or believe it, but the Lord is my refuge. No evil will befall me. God said so. If you've ever taken anything seriously in your life, please take this seriously. I trust God. I hope and pray one day you will trust Him too. Until then, you need to know that He doesn't close His eyes to your evil intentions."

"Now, that truly hurt my feelings. Evil intentions? That really hurt." Matt clutched his chest as if mortally wounded. "God really told you that?"

"You think this is a joke, but everyone has to answer for their sins. Sins have consequences—death and punishment from God. If you hear nothing else I say, please take Him seriously."

"Well, not that I am keeping score—," Matt placed his hands back on his hips, "—but so far, it looks like I'm ahead." He winked at

Eliana, then frowned. "But, let me get this straight. Are you saying you will ask God to punish me for my so-called evil intentions? Hmm. That sounds like a threat to me." He looked at Kirstie, his eyes sparkling bright.

Eliana shook her head, and turned away from them. *Lord, speak to their hardened hearts.*

~~

"Hi, Mom."

"Hi, sweetie."

"I'm home. Do you have time to talk?"

"Of course. Did you find out anything about the note?"

"Unfortunately, I did. It's complicated, but you can assume that deal is off. I'm sorry."

"I had hoped you found out something different. That was a good offer. Without that—"

"I'm sorry, Mom. We'll figure out something. If I have to, I'll come back and take over the business. I plan to take the bar in a few months and we can make plans after that."

"I'll be fine. You just do what the Lord leads you to do. He'll take care of us. Don't worry; just pray about it. That's my advice to myself, too."

"Good advice for us both. I love you, Mom."

"I love you too, sweetheart."

~~

Friday

As soon as Eliana arrived, Julie pointed to Abram's door. "He wants to see you ASAP."

Eliana tapped at the door, and Abram responded, "Come in."

Abram pointed to the chair and Eliana sat. His steely eyes and folded arms across his chest informed her this would not end well.

Eliana's pulse quickened and her head throbbed.

"Eliana, I thought a lot of Milton. He and I went back a long way. I counted on him to be a sounding board with the conservative arguments, and that's what I expected from you. Sure, he held onto some religious views, but he never crossed the line with them. I respected him for talking about his beliefs, then for the most part, knowing when to shut up. Evidently you didn't inherit that from him. I could overlook the harassment deal with Matt, but I won't overlook threats."

"Threats, sir?"

He pulled a file from in front of him and slapped it on the desk toward Eliana. "Yes. Threats. Matt reported to HR yesterday that you threatened him with retaliation from God. This is serious business, young lady. I already warned you, and now you leave me no more options. You will pack up your things and leave. Now." He flung his hands with a sweeping motion toward the door.

Two uniformed security men waited at Eliana's desk. One instructed her, "Pick up only your personal belongings and come with us."

Humiliation hammered at Eliana's temples.

Julie focused on her computer screen.

After she picked up her computer satchel and purse, the men from security each held one of Eliana's elbows and escorted her out of the office. They led her past curious employees who moved to the side and whispered.

When they reached a security checkpoint, Eliana went through a scanner while another guard rifled through her purse and satchel. When they were sure she'd taken nothing from the building, they confiscated her security and parking passes, and led her to the parking garage exit.

Only a few steps into the parking garage, she spotted her bicycle, now with cardboard angel wings taped on the back fender. As she pulled them off, she prayed. *God, make Yourself real to Matt. I forgive them, all of them, and just ask that somehow they will see that You are real and trust in You.*

~~

"Mom, I'm coming home." Eliana's sweaty palm threatened to lose its grip on the phone.

"Great! I always enjoy our visits."

"Well, it's more than a visit. I'm not going back to D.C. I lost my job today."

"What happened, honey?"

"I'll tell you about it when I come home. I'll pack up here tonight and close out the lease tomorrow. I should be able to drive back home by Sunday."

"I'm so sorry. I know that job meant a lot to you."

"It meant a lot to Granddaddy. That's what hurts the most. It was the last gift he gave me, and I threw it away."

"Don't say that. You just pack up and get home safely, and we'll sort it out. I love you, and I'm very proud of you. He was too. Be careful. I'll see you soon."

"I love you. See you Sunday. Bye."

God, I always felt You set me on this path into law, and even into this job. What do I do wrong?

Where do I go from here?

If the accusations Matt made against me stay on my record ... What do I do?

I need to hear from You, Lord.

~~

Exhausted from the emotions of the day and her brain overloaded with details of moving so quickly, Eliana collapsed on her bed long after midnight.

God, I feel like a failure. Help me. Show me. Her consciousness drifted to an ivory and golden room. *This has to be another dream. It's Ahab's palace again.*

Elijah spoke again, "King Ahab. I have come to let you know YHWH has been patient with your idol worship. But you must realize this turning away from Almighty God will bring judgment."

Ahab dismissed him. "Didn't Moses already warn us in the Torah that the rain would cease and the land would not give forth its produce, if we should worship other gods? Yet, nothing has happened as of yet."

Elijah nodded. "Because of His lovingkindness and mercy. You don't even recognize that. Now you will see that not merely shall Moses' words, but mine also will be fulfilled. As surely as the LORD, the God of Israel lives—" he paused to restrain his emotions "—before whom I stand," his courage swelled at the reminder, "there will be neither dew nor rain these years, except by my word."

Elijah jerked his arms away from the guards and strode out of the room, unhindered.

By the time Ahab shouted, "Be gone," Elijah had already set his feet on the street again.

The townspeople taunted him. "Tell us about your important meeting with the king. It didn't last very long."

"Tell us, did he see your finery and request a ride to the next town? Or, did he appoint you to his court? No? Did he offer you a fine robe to replace this thing or perhaps a nose ring to bring you into his stable? Go back to the desert, you camel."

The mob slapped at his mantle to push him along the path. Mothers pulled their children near to protect them from the hostile throng.

The taunts escalated. Elijah's heart pounded, his palms sweat, his lungs couldn't get enough air, "YHWH! Where are You? Don't let me die at the hand of this mob that Ahab's gods will be glorified."

I know God will help him, as He helped me.

Invisible walls divided them into two groups, and the crowd separated. Elijah passed between them with no one able to touch him. The LORD spoke to him as he walked in the midst of the people, supernaturally restrained from harming him. "Go away from here and turn eastward, and hide yourself by the brook Cherith, which is east of the Jordan. There, you will drink of the brook, and I have commanded the ravens to provide for you there."

"Yes, LORD. Yes. I will do as You have said. I beg You, let my people see that you alone are God Almighty."

The same dream as before. Elijah left. Today, You had me leave too?

Eliana heard Elijah speak, now at the brook Cherith. "I showed myself to King Ahab, now I am to hide myself. But even King David hid from Saul. As long as You are with me, Adonai, I will not be afraid."

I am not afraid, Lord. I trust You.

Elijah strolled along the sandy edges of brook Cherith, a seasonal wadi that fed into the Jordan river—a perfect place to hide. He walked toward a small rock ledge over an opening. Under the ledge appeared a nice shaded spot, just right for him to rest. In the level ground there, he spread out his mantle to form a cushion for his head, removed his sandals, and patted them together to shake loose the dirt. Isolated, even desolate, but safe. No one would find him here.

As God promised, a raven swooped in and landed near him. The black bird tucked his wings behind him and strutted to the entrance of the shelter, his lustrous feathers sparkling with every muscle movement. He dropped a cake of flat bread on a stone by Elijah and spoke, "Elohim sends this to you."

Amazing. God, You are so amazing. Eliana settled into the dream as if watching a movie.

Elijah answered. "Well, I expected you, but I didn't expect you to speak. Thank you, Oreb. You are a faithful servant to our LORD." Elijah picked up the bread and raised it to the sky, giving thanks to the LORD who provides.

"Oh, Adonai, Elohim, Yehovah-Jireh. You see me and provide for me. You also see the uncleanness and evil within your people. Stretch out Your mighty hand again, that Your people will see and know that You alone, are El Elyon, Most High. As You took hold of this unclean bird to bring me nourishment, take hold of Your unclean people. Show them Your righteousness that they will again look to You. Withhold the rain that Jezebel seeks from her evil gods. Withhold the rain, that they will know when it comes that it comes from You. Withhold the rain so when they see You provide it, they will turn from their wickedness and remember You are their God."

The raven took one hop then lifted into flight. Elijah ate the cake, amazed at the unusual quality of it. He knelt by the brook to scoop out a few handfuls of water and drank from the brook Cherith, as God commanded.

Another group of ravens came to Elijah and left meat for him. He thanked them and expressed his gratefulness for the tasty food they brought to him.

One raven replied, "It should be tasty. Elohim instructed us to take it from the king's table."

God does have a sense of humor.

Elijah laughed out loud at the thought of ravens swooping in and stealing from Ahab's banquet table to bring food to him. "The God of Israel taking food from the king of Israel's table. If he doesn't repent and turn from the worship of foreign gods, more than table scraps will be taken from him."

Eliana watched snippets of Elijah's days, worshipping El Elyon. Mornings and evenings, the orebs brought him bread and meat. He drank from the brook and took shelter under a rocky shelf. The prophet agonized over the evilness of the king and his kinsmen, rejoiced in the lovingkindness of his God, and fervently beseeched YHWH to withhold rain, so that His people would turn to back to Him.

In the mornings, Elijah went into the brook to wash his limbs and face. The scorching heat compelled him to return to the rocky shelter within minutes. So, he sat alone and waited for the orebs. Waited for a word from God. He pleaded for his people.

He pleaded.

He waited.

He listened.

After a few months, the seasonal rains came no longer to refresh the wadi. Instead of rinsing his arms and legs each morning, Elijah found only enough water to dip his fingers in a puddle and used that to moisten his cracked lips.

He must feel so alone.

Eliana heard Elijah's thoughts as if he said them aloud. He remembered how the children of Israel complained against God and accused Him of bringing them into the desert to die. When he heard the stories as a child, it sounded preposterous that a people who witnessed the hand of YHWH perform such miracles would doubt Him.

Now he was in a wilderness, totally dependent on God's provision. The fear was his own, and it was real. The LORD told me to come here. He provided meat and bread, but there is no more water. The ravens can't bring that to me. I trust You; I do, O, LORD. I just don't see You. I haven't heard from You. I don't mind dying for You, O, LORD, but please let me die in service to You, not here hiding.

The words of the Psalm of David pierced his doubt and fear as it played in his thoughts. "The angel of the LORD encamps around those who fear Him, and rescues them. O taste and see that the LORD is good; How blessed is the man who takes refuge in Him! O fear the LORD, you His saints; for to those who fear Him there is no want. The young lions do lack and suffer hunger; but they who seek the LORD shall not be in want of any good thing."

I trust You, O LORD. You have sustained me these many days. You alone. You are encamped here with me. You are my refuge. You will rescue me now in my thirst. I trust You to show me what to do. Show me.

That's my prayer too. LORD, show me what to do.

The word of the LORD came to Elijah and said, "Arise, go to Zarephath, which belongs to Sidon, and stay there; behold, I have commanded a widow there to provide for you."

Zarephath, west of the Jordan on the Mediterranean coast. How many days, no, how many weeks would it take to walk that far? Will there be water along the way? Jezebel's father Ethbaal, ruled there. He had killed the previous king to take his place. Baal worshippers. Evil Baal worshippers. God Almighty is going to provide for me under Ethbaal's nose, in the middle of pagans. Brilliant.

"How appropriate that the God of Abraham, Isaac, and Jacob would use another helpless one to provide a place for me in the middle of pagans, that they may know that He is God."

Oreb interrupted the prophet. "Are you talking to me?"

Startled by the voice, Elijah chuckled. "No. I didn't realize you were here. I was just thinking out loud. Elohim is moving me from here to Zarephath, so I will be leaving now. Thank you for bringing me food every day."

The raven nodded. "I am obedient to Elohim."

Elijah replied, "That is my desire too, my friend." He stood, shook the dust from his mantle, tossed it around his shoulders, picked up his staff, and headed west toward the Jordan. Surely the Jordan still flowed. There, he would drink, cross over to the west, and then head north to Zarephath.

Then the dream shifted back to the palace. Ahab was seated, and Jezebel came into the room. She complimented her husband on the fine workmanship of the temples he built, especially the ivory pillar to Astarte. "My king, my husband." She curtsied and extended her hand.

He took it and drew her nearer to his throne. "Yes, dear Queen."

"You have kept your promise to build the temples to my gods, and they are magnificent. Thank you, my love."

"I am glad you are pleased."

"I am but …"

"But what?"

"But there are still those priests of the house of Levi who speak out against them. Against me. When we gather to worship our gods and pray to the lord over all the weather, the lightning, the rain our land needs, these Levite priests harass us and make claims against us as if their god is the only god. We are simply worshipping our god and seeking his favor. I only want to help bring prosperity to this land and our people."

Ahab pressed one hand against his temple.

Elijah's warning is giving him a headache.

"My king," Jezebel continued, "all I ask is that they be quieted so I may worship without harassment. If I can tolerate their old god, why shouldn't they tolerate my gods? I only want to worship my gods in peace so that we may have the prosperity the people expect from you."

Jezebel knelt at his side, leaned in close to him, and spoke in a near whisper while she traced over his hand with one finger. "You have seen how I ornament my body with intricate henna and luscious honey before I worship. You always enjoy the colorful lilies, fragrant roses, sweet cakes, and honey I gather to wear and take for offerings. I will come to you first, before I make my offering to the prince of the earth. If you are pleased, I will then go to the temple and pray that the gods bring life to the wadis again. I will ask that Astarte will be pleased to fill my womb with your children. My desire is to always to please you."

With Ahab fully entranced with her beauty, she leaned back from him and said, "My king, I know you have many important tasks before you. I will not ask you to waste your time on this. If you give the order, I will see to it and will not trouble you with it. If you wish, my king."

He reached out his hand and she placed hers within it. "Go ahead. Do as you like with them. And bring yourself to me before you go to worship."

Jezebel nodded and raised both eyebrows at his request. She twirled her skirt and turned back to see if Ahab watched. When he did, she flashed him a quick smile.

Jezebel marched toward her quarters and barked orders to the staff to find all the prophets of the LORD. "My father killed the king before him to take his place. Why should I not eliminate some troublesome prophets?"

Eliana woke, her heart racing. *God moved Elijah, not to his home, but to a remote area. If I move in with Mom, will I put my family in danger? I know what Matt did. Does he see me as a threat? How far would he go to seek revenge and keep his career unstained?*

Lisa Worthey Smith

Chapter Six

Sunday morning

"Mom."

"Hi sweetie. Are you on your way?"

"I'm packed up and leaving in a few minutes, but I'm not coming to your house right away."

"I have your room ready, so whenever you get here will be fine. We're about to head to church."

"Thanks, Mom. I … I don't think I will be there today."

"Going to do some sight-seeing?"

What do I tell her? I don't want her to be frightened.

"Honey, are you okay?"

"I am. I need to get away for a little while. I might go visit a college friend."

"Well, some friend left you a package during the night. It didn't come through the mail, I found it on my porch this morning when I went out to get the paper."

"What kind of package, Mom. Did you open it?"

"No. It's a nice gift bag with a small, velvety box inside. Probably a gift congratulating you on your new job. Want me to open it?"

"It isn't ticking or anything, is it?"

Grace laughed. "Of course not. I'll go get it and open it while I have you on the phone. Hold on. I'll put you on speaker so I can use both hands and still talk. The box has a little rattle to it. It might have come from a jewelry store. It's very pretty. Oh. Oh, dear."

"What, Mom? What is it? Are you okay?"

"It's pearls, or at least they used to be pearls. Why would someone paint them black? No, it isn't paint. They're charred. It's a pearl necklace that has been burned. Sweetheart, I don't like this. What's going on? Are you in danger?"

Eliana's throat thickened. "It's probably just a joke. Some people at work made fun of my pearls. That's all. You and Johnny enjoy your church service. I'll check in with you later. Love you." Eliana swiped to end the call and immediately called Johnny.

"Hey, kiddo."

"Hey, sis. You on your way home?"

"Actually, I'm not. Are you away from Mom? Can she hear you?"

"No. I mean yeah, I'm in my room."

"Good. Did she tell you about the package on the porch?"

"Yeah, she told me. Was it a graduation gift or something?"

"It wasn't that kind of a gift. It was more of a threat. I can't go into it right now, but just keep your eye on things. Watch the house, watch Mom. Just in case—"

"Is there a hit out on us or something?"

"I'm not joking, Johnny. You could be in real danger. You and Mom. Because of me. I don't have time to go into it right now. Don't tell Mom. She has enough to worry about right now. Promise me."

"Sure. Promise. But you need to tell me. How do I know what to be careful of if I don't know what's going on?"

"I'll check in later. It's almost time for church, and you need to—"

"manage your time wisely. Yeah, I am. Love you, sis. Be careful."

Ping. Text from Mom. "*We got cut off. I love you, Eliana, and know that God intends to use you as He told me He would. Mom.*"

You have no idea. He is doing something, but I don't know what yet. Abram isn't king Ahab, but he has a lot of power. Plenty of Jezebels enticing and manipulating. Blinded and blinding others into ungodly paths and awful decisions.

Ping. From Julie. "*Watch your back. Call me when you can. I'm going to miss you.*"

To Julie. "*Have time to talk now?*"

Ping. From Julie. "*Sure.*"

Eliana dialed Julie's phone number. "Hi, Julie. Are you okay? How's Emma?"

"So good to hear your voice. I'm fine. Emma's better, thanks. I was just worried about you. Friday, after you left, Matt spent a good bit of time in Abram's office, and as Matt left, Abram asked for your mom's address. I wrote it on a piece of paper, and he handed it to Matt. They are both up to something. I just wanted to give you a head's up."

"You were right. Someone delivered a package to my mom's house for me. It was a box of burned pearls."

"Oh, dear."

"Did you hear them say anything about me? Do you have any idea what it means? I know Matt wasn't happy that I turned down his advances. Just what should I expect from him after all he's done already?"

"He's totally thrilled that he got you fired. I think he's warning you not to disclose what really happened. His family has strong connections to Abram, and they have a way of eliminating anything that tarnishes or threatens their combined empire. You'd be surprised to learn of the convenient suicides, car accidents, and missing persons among their enemies, whether perceived or real."

"Are you saying he would go so far as to physically hurt me? Or hurt my family?" Eliana waited several seconds for an answer. "Julie? Are you there?"

"I shouldn't say too much."

"Are you safe there?"

"Yes, I will be as long as I play along and keep my mouth shut. This call is my first transgression, so please don't tell anyone. They wouldn't hesitate—"

"I promise. I won't say anything. I'm so sorry you have to live like this."

"I also wanted to thank you for your concern about Emma. I know I dismissed your 'prayer' idea, but the next day she was much better. So, if you prayed some magic prayer, thank you."

"There's nothing magic about it. I did pray to the God of the universe and so did my mom. He hears our prayers. He loves you, Julie. He really does."

"From what I've heard, He wouldn't love me knowing what I have done."

"You mean the abortion?"

"Yes."

"But He *does* love you, even knowing every single sin. No one is sinless. I'm certainly not. That's why He took the punishment for our sins. He loves us and wants you and me to spend eternity with Him."

"I appreciate that. I know you mean well. I do admire your faith and how you didn't cave to the couch-hopping around here."

"I don't behave a certain way to gain anyone's admiration. I hope you know that."

"I didn't mean that at all. You truly act on what you believe. It was refreshing to be around someone who dealt honestly instead of saying or doing what they thought was expected."

"I definitely disappointed them in that arena. You probably heard that the clerks called me Purity in Pearls."

"Yeah. I could think of a few names to call them."

"Well, thank you for the warning. I appreciate it, Julie. If you don't mind, I'd like to pray with you before we hang up."

"I, uh, I really don't know much about that—"

"How about I pray for us both?"

"Okay. That works."

"Dear Father. Thank You for providing me this friend in the midst of a hostile situation. Thank You for her courage and perseverance. Please be with her in the coming days. Please grant her a measure of peace as she deals with unscrupulous people. Grant her direction and wisdom with her husband and daughter. Protect them, Lord. Draw them near to You and let Your presence be known to them. Show me exactly what You want me to do, and give me strength and courage to do it, no matter the cost. I pray in Jesus' name, amen."

"Amen. Sorry. Am I supposed to say 'amen' too?"

"If you want to. The word 'amen' means 'so be it.' So, if you agree, then 'amen' is appropriate."

"I'm lucky to have you as a friend too, Eliana. Thank you for praying for us. I hope we can keep in touch. Where are you going?"

"I planned to go to Mom's house, but now I am giving that second thoughts. I don't want to put her or my brother in any danger."

"It may sound like a wacky idea, but Todd and I have a little cabin a couple of hours from here along the Shenandoah. It belonged to his parents, and we inherited it when they died a few years ago. We only use it when Todd needs to escape from the city. If you want a secluded spot, no one at work knows about it. I can meet you and give you directions and keys."

"It sounds exactly like what I have been praying for and what God has been showing me. A secluded place by the water. If you are sure Todd won't mind, I'm very interested in it."

"I'll go ask him. Hang on."

God. I don't want to intrude on Julie. I want to follow You. Please let Todd have no reservations if You want me to go. If he does have reservations, I will know You don't want me to go.

"Eliana? You still there?"

"I'm here."

"Todd said he's heard me talk of you and he has no reservations about letting you stay there, as long as you like."

"He literally said 'no reservations'?"

"Yeah. Why?"

"That's exactly how I asked God to answer. 'Let Todd have no reservations, if God wanted me to use the cabin.'"

"You prayed and received an answer just like that?"

"Yes. And if the offer is still on the table, I'll meet you for the keys and details at your convenience."

"Good. I am so glad to be able to help. How about the coffee shop around the corner from the courthouse? Thirty minutes work for you?"

"Perfect. I'll be there. Thank you so much. And thank Todd, too."

~~

Luray, Virginia

Just what I needed, Lord. The Shenandoah Valley showcases the magnificence of Your creation. The John Denver song had it right about those Blue Ridge mountains and almost heaven.

Eliana found the mom-and-pop grocery store that Julie recommended in Luray, a quaint town with a population of about five thousand. She bought enough supplies to last a week or more, and then drove the final few miles to the cabin.

She pulled into the driveway, rolled down her windows and inhaled the vibrant evergreens that lined the gravel drive. As the gravel crunched below her car, she took in the beauty of it all. A rustic log cabin with a metal roof and a great view of the valley from the front. Eliana walked around back and gazed at the river tripping over smooth rocks along the edge of the back yard. The sounds and verdant greens of life here all soothed her spirit.

What a contrast from the concrete and exhaust fumes from the city traffic. No wonder Julie and Todd come here to relax.

She circled back to the front and unlocked the front door. Inside, she marveled at the gathering room with its rock fireplace. Around the corner, she discovered a small galley-style kitchen with a breakfast nook. One bedroom and one bath just beyond the gathering room completed the picture. *Perfect. Thank You, Father.*

Eliana made a couple of trips to and from her car for her groceries. She set them on the counter and settled in. *I can study for the bar in peace, and keep Mom and Johnny out of danger. Hmm. I'd better let them know where I am, without letting them know where I am.*

She wandered around with her phone trying to find a place with a good signal.

Kitchen, no.

Living room, no.

Back deck, one, sometimes two bars if she turned directly south. Eliana dialed her mom, inhaled the sweet honeysuckle and privet blooms, and waited.

"Mom?"

"Eliana is that you? This isn't a good connection."

"It's me, Mom. How are you? Everything okay?"

"We're fine. We still have no takers on Moore and Barrington, but something will work out. How are you? Where are you? Some of your friends have called, trying to find you."

"What did you tell them?"

"What you told me, that you might go visit a college friend."

"That's good."

"Which friend are you with? One of the sorority girls?"

"No. Who called wanting to find me?"

"They didn't leave their names; just that they were your friends and wanted to see you."

"I don't want you to worry."

"Well, when you say it like that, now I *am* worried."

"I need to tell you some things. It's a little complicated, but the law firm backing out and the burned pearls are tied together. I ruffled some feathers at work; now these people want to make sure I don't ruffle anymore."

"That sounds ominous. Ruffling feathers isn't your style."

"Like I said, it's complicated. I'm not coming home right now, and you can tell anyone who calls that much. I don't want them bothering you. Just know that I'm safe in a place where no one knows me. I'll settle in here, study for the bar, and see where God leads me from here."

"So, you aren't going to tell me where you are?"

"I'll give you a hint. Think of what you named me, and after whom. Think of the story with the ravens, and it should give you a little idea without saying too much over the phone."

Grace whispered. "Our phone is bugged?"

"It's possible, so please don't say or ask any more."

Call ended. No signal.

Eliana's shoulders sagged. *I don't want her to worry or be afraid. Lord, if You are going to use me as You used Elijah, prepare me and direct me for Your purpose.*

~~

Eliana ambled down to the river. The water refreshing and relaxing, she sat on the rocky edge and let her feet dangle in the cool water. She took deep breaths of the clean air. *I almost forgot the smell of clean air.* She imagined it cleaning all the frustration out of her heart. *God I am trusting You. I need to hear You.*

A yellow butterfly flitted from across the river toward her. Eliana held out her hand, and it lit in her palm. The dainty creature stayed with her for a couple of minutes, crawling from the front to the back of her hand with the slightest of tickle to Eliana's skin.

While entranced with the butterfly, the Lord spoke in her mind. *I created this butterfly. You may see it as weak, but I can use it for My purpose to do powerful things. See the magnificent colors and pattern? To you, it looks like all the butterflies of its kind, yet I created and prepared this particular one for this day, so it would come to you. Eliana, all its life, it did what ordinary butterflies do, without knowing how I would use it. I only told it of its mission a moment ago. If I can use this tiny creature to do great things, and it trusts Me, you can too.*

"Oh, Lord, thank You. I do trust You. Thank You for calming my heart." The butterfly took flight and bobbed among the yellow and pink wildflowers along the riverbank before disappearing.

Eliana remembered the light touch and the gentle feel of the butterfly on her hand. *What an amazing moment. Isn't that just like God to demonstrate His sovereignty and power with something so weak?*

Eliana meandered barefoot on the cool grass, to the cabin and sorted through the groceries again. She laid out some bread and chips for a light sandwich. The soft drinks and sliced turkey chilled in the refrigerator. Before she put together her dinner, she closed every curtain and window blind and checked the front and back door locks.

After enjoying her sandwich, Eliana relaxed and surveyed the gathering room. The coffee table had smooth ridges along the length of the top, suggesting hand-planing. *Probably some of Todd's work.* Her fingers followed the long smooth ridges. The chairs in the kitchen seemed to be the same wood. *So much beautiful woodwork here. He does really nice work.*

The wind whistled through the logs, and Eliana jerked around to see if someone were in the room with her. The whistle came again along with the rustle of the trees outside.

Calm down.

Breathe.

Only Julie and Todd know I'm here.

With no "city noise," every creak of the house startled her during the night. Her head pounded. She opened her eyes often to look for unwanted guests and clenched the blanket near her chin until her hands ached.

I'm letting my imagination get the best of me. I was so brave a little while ago. Who am I to fear? No one. God is with me; He is for me. He has placed me here for a reason, and I will trust Him.

Her heart believed it, but her head still considered the possibility of danger with every sound.

If I disappeared now, no one except Julie would know where I am.

I paid cash for the gas and groceries. There was nothing to trace.

Except the phone call.

Would they go to those lengths to find her? To eliminate her?

~~

Monday morning

Julie pressed the intercom to Abram's office. "Matt to see you, Your Honor."

She glanced at him. "Go in. He will see you."

Matt closed the door behind him and stood near Abram's desk. "Sir. Purity's cell phone pinged over the weekend near the Shenandoah river. She's running."

"Hmm. Any known contacts there? Family?"

"Not family, but Julie has a place there. They talked after she left here."

"Plant some eyes in the area, and keep me posted. We'll flush her out."

"Yes, sir."

"She's a loose cannon we don't want to explode. If she goes digging into Milton's death—"

"Yes, sir."

"And, Your Honor, how do you want the rest of her family handled? Want us to go ahead with the plan?"

"Not yet. Let's see how it plays out."

"Yes, sir."

"Good work, Matt."

~~

In the early morning hours, Eliana had finally submitted to a light sleep. When she woke, it was nearly nine a.m. Eliana tiptoed barefoot into the kitchen to make some coffee to caffeinate her headache. She peered through bloodshot eyes over the sparkling river. A couple of wood ducks floated in the current, swerving to avoid the rocks and bobbing their heads for small fish.

All calm.

No ax murderers in sight, then again, they would hide, wouldn't they? My head hurts too much to laugh at my own jokes.

She pulled back the front curtain and watched a few deer grazing in the dewy meadow.

If they aren't spooked, I guess nothing is amiss. Nothing roaming around except the wind.

She surveyed everything within view from the window. No, her car was car parked out front. *Great. I forgot every murder mystery movie I ever watched. Why did I leave my car out front? Everyone knows the bad guys will look for the car. I should have parked it behind the cabin.*

Eliana grabbed a power bar from the kitchen and peeled open the wrapper. Maybe that would hold her headache at survival level until the coffee was ready. While she chewed, she pulled on some sweat pants and a tee shirt. She picked up her car keys and checked out the front window again before opening the front door.

The deer were gone, but a car parked in the street near the front of the cabin.

A light blue Focus.

The driver studied her car and held his phone to his ear.

Eliana's heart clamored and tried to squeeze her throat. Her headache took all her brain cells hostage. *What do I do? I have no weapons here. Lord, protect me.*

The driver nodded, ended his phone call, and then drove away. Eliana's heartbeat pounded in her eardrums and behind her eyes.

Exhausted, she leaned against the door frame. *Lord, You told my mother You wanted to use me. You have brought me to this place. You have given me dreams of Elijah. If this is my brook Cherith experience, I will count on You to protect me. You reminded me of Your plan with the butterfly. You have guided my steps this far. I trust You to lead me from here.*

She took a deep breath of Holy Spirit courage, exhaled her fears, tossed her keys in the air, then caught them with a swagger.

Whom shall I fear?

Her car crunched the gravel along the drive to the back of the cabin where she parked it near the deck, facing the road in case she needed a fast getaway. *I do remember that much.*

Her coffee ready, she poured a cup and sat at the counter inhaling the rich aroma while it cooled. *Murder. I have to consider the possibility that these guys are capable of murder. If Julie is right, they are already guilty, so it wouldn't be a big deal to them to add one more to their list. If they have so much influence and power, why would they worry about me revealing what Matt did to me? Wouldn't that be a slap-on-the-hand offense to them?*

I wish I could talk to Granddaddy. I wish he could tell me why he requested I work with Abram.

Eliana jumped when a ping from her phone interrupted.

From Johnny. *Sis. U ok?*

To Johnny. *Yes. How are you?*

Ping. *Mom's cleaning out the law office. Going through some of Granddaddy's papers. Having a hard time with it. She seems spooked about something. Are you coming home soon?*

Tell Mom to keep all the papers, appointment books, notebooks, I want them all.

Ping. *OK. Any particular reason?*

No. Just sentimental.

Ping. *What's she all worked up about?*

Can't say, kiddo. What are you doing this summer? Ready for University of Virginia?

Ping. *Ready as I will ever B. I get 2 use my charm skills on a whole new crop of college girls.*

What about you and Bella?

Ping. *She's history. Going 2 some Ivy League school 2 marry money."*

I need to go study. Love you! Keep your eye on Mom.

Ping. *Love U 2, sis. Will do.*

~~

Eliana texted Julie. *I know you are at work, but when you have time, please text or call.*

After lunch, Julie called. "Hi. Everything okay?"

"Thanks for calling. I won't keep you long. First, thank you for the use of the cabin. It's perfect. Todd has some beautiful woodwork here. Tell him he is really talented."

"Sure. I'll tell him. He takes great pride in that."

"Back when Abram talked with my granddaddy, do you know what they talked about? Did he keep any records of that?"

"I think the last time I put him through to Abram was about a month or so before you came to work here. I don't know what they discussed, but I remember he and Matt stayed in private conference all that afternoon."

"Thanks for everything. The place is great, but I might go home, unannounced, for a day or two. Anyone questioning about me or my whereabouts?"

"Actually, yes. Abram pulled your personnel file and he had Matt check into your law school and local references. Kirstie and Shally both tried to pump me for information. Be careful."

"I will. Thanks again. Bye." *How stupid. I was so careful with Johnny, then just let anyone listening know where I am and where I am going. I'm way too tired to think straight.*

~~

During the drive home, Eliana focused on her family. *Grandma in her own little world. Mom, grieving over another tremendous loss and trying to figure out how to manage financially without the firm. Johnny. Dear Johnny. He has college ahead of him and no direction whatsoever at the moment. Strictly driven by the wind. Father, touch his heart. Remind him of the promise he made a few years ago to live for You.*

Eliana pulled her car to the back of her childhood home and opened the back door into the kitchen. "Mom? You home? Johnny?"

"Hi, sweetie." Mom came to the kitchen from the front of the house. "I thought I heard a car, but when I reached the front door, I didn't see anyone. Where did you park?"

"Around back this time. How are you?"

"I'm great. How are you?"

"Wonderful. Johnny said you have gone through some of Granddaddy's things. May I take a look?"

"Sure. He told me you wanted me to save them all." Grace whispered, "can we talk or is the house bugged?"

Eliana gave her a squeeze. "We're okay."

"I put everything in your room. Come on, I'll show you." Grace paused when the phone rang. "Let me get that. It's probably for you. Someone calls once or twice a day for you. You want to get it, since you're here?"

"No. If it is for me, just tell them I'm not here. I know you don't normally lie—"

"Hello? Yes?" Grace grimaced and looked at Eliana. "No, she's not here. I don't know. Do you want to leave a message? Who should I say is calling? Hello?"

"I guess this is where they hang up on you?"

"Yes. Every time. Weird."

"The papers?"

"Yes, I put them in your chest of drawers. The case files are still at the office. These were the documents in his desk."

"Okay. I'll go look through them. You don't have to come."

"Then I'll put together some dinner. Johnny should be home soon."

"Did he take that summer job at the rec center?"

"Yes. He hates it, but he needed some spending money for school this fall."

Eliana pulled out the drawers to find stacks of folders, address books, and planners. They smelled of Grandaddy's office and his cologne.

Granddaddy. She held his planner as if it were a portal to him, and caressed the monogrammed M on the front. *I miss you. I miss your voice. The way you said my name, as if it were the richest name in all the world, and I were some precious jewel. I wish you could tell me about Abram. I wish I could tell you about my experience there.*

She gave the planner a pat and put it aside to look for his correspondence files. Eliana fingered through the most recent ones. In the weeks before he died, there was no letter addressed to Abram. She pulled the letters out of the folder and lifted each one to see if she missed a page.

Nothing. *I'll ask Mom about it tomorrow.*

~~

Tuesday

The smell of bacon woke Eliana. She shuffled the papers on top of her to the side. *I must have fallen asleep going through Granddaddy's things.* Eliana pulled a robe around her and wandered to the kitchen. "Good morning. Smells wonderful in here." She slipped her arms around her mom's waist and hugged her.

"Well, good morning to you, sweetie. Sleep well? You were conked out the last time I checked in on you."

"Yes, thank you. Guess I was more tired than I realized." Eliana opened the cabinet and pulled out a mug. "Do you remember sending a letter of recommendation for me to work with Abram?" She chose a Columbian Blend coffee pod and dropped it in the machine.

"No, sweetie. Your granddaddy really didn't want you to do that. He wanted you to work with him. I thought you must have applied on your own and used him as a reference."

"And every piece of his correspondence is copied and should be in the documents you brought home?" The coffee maker gurgled out the last drop and Eliana tossed the empty pod.

"Should be."

Eliana stood beside her mother, as she carefully turned each strip of bacon in the skillet. "What about email? Could he have sent an email?"

"It's possible, I guess. But I usually did all that too, and printed a copy to file." Grace transferred the crispy bacon to a paper-lined plate and pulled the carton of eggs closer.

"I never knew Granddaddy to text, so I guess it's pointless to ask about that possibility."

Grace tilted her head back and chuckled. "He refused to learn anything about texting. Your grandfather had enough challenges keeping up with emails and cell phones."

"Can you sign me into his personal email account, not the one for Moore and Barrington? Would you mind if I looked at his emails?"

"I don't mind. How about after breakfast? I'm almost finished here. Johnny should be ready any minute."

Eliana bent over to look in the oven. "It looks like the biscuits still need a few minutes. Could you give me the passwords so I can look while you finish here?"

"Sure." Grace stepped over to a desk and jotted his computer and email sign-in information on a sticky note. She passed it to Eliana. "I'll need to finish up here. These are the passwords you'll need."

"Thanks, Mom."

Eliana found emails to and from Abram. She scrolled to the dates about a month before he died and pulled them up, one at a time.

Most had to do with a time to call or return a call to one or the other.

Two weeks before he died, he emailed Abram. "We've been friends far too long for me to let this slide. You can't make a deal with the devil and not expect to pay the price. I beg you. Do not be a part of this. I'm praying for you, friend. I pray God will touch your heart so you will see the evil of this, and not be enticed into it."

Eliana pressed *print* and moved to the next one.

From Abram. "I can always arrange for your granddaughter to come work for me. I can introduce her to all kinds of people. She might like it here."

Milton's reply. "No. I will absolutely not allow her to work there. We already discussed this." *Print.*

The most current email, dated the day before Milton died.

From Abram. "I can and I will, but out of courtesy to you, and because of our long friendship, I prefer to give you the opportunity to agree voluntarily, rather than take extreme measures."

From Milton. "Friendship or not, I am obligated to report this to the authorities." *Print.*

Think I'll forward them to my email, just to be safe.

Granddaddy knew something. Abram took extreme measures, killed him, or had him killed. He must have manufactured the letter of request for me to work there. That's why I received the call out of the blue.

Eliana's stomach sickened.

Why did Abram hire me for special research? All the clerks researched case law for rulings. What did he want from me? Why did Granddaddy try to protect me? What did he know? What was he going to report?

Johnny's face peeked around the door. "Hey, Sis. I didn't expect to see you. What are you doin'? You all right?" He sat on the corner of the desk and studied her face. "What's wrong?"

Eliana shook her head, afraid if she spoke, her insides would surely churn out of her.

"Mom has breakfast ready. She sent me to get you."

She motioned for him to go ahead. "I'll be right there."

What did he mean by 'deal with the devil'? Abram had me look at the church sermon, abortion, then some school cases involving Muslims and Buddhists. Were these the issues he asked Granddaddy about too? What kind of advice did he give? Did it have to do with ruling on a case? But Abram couldn't be reported for his rulings, so what did he plan to do that Granddaddy would report?

It's pretty clear Markham came to 'entice' him to keep the abortion laws as they are. If Granddaddy knew about this, Abram would probably receive a reprimand, but would that be enough for him to risk murder?

Was it the religion in schools issue? Was there a "lobbyist" there I didn't see? Who did he make a deal with? How was Matt involved? His family's in politics and legal circles. I need to find out more about them. Maybe the answer is there. Eliana's head swirled with possibilities, but nothing made sense.

Ping. From Julie. *Are you okay? Please text ASAP.*

To Julie. *Hi, I'm fine. Has something happened?*

Ping. From Julie. *Local police called. The cabin is burning. They can't save it.*

Lisa Worthey Smith

Chapter Seven

Eliana's stomach served her well through leftover pizza in college and law school, but it never had to deal with intensity of this level. Until now, she never had to give her queasy stomach such strict commands to cooperate.

She mustered a pleasant disguise on her face before she arrived in the kitchen. "Mom, Johnny, you really need to take a trip to the Hamptons and visit Dad's parents."

"Honey, what are you talking about?"

"No." Eliana bustled around the kitchen so she could avoid their eyes. "Better yet. I'll book you a place in the city. Then you can sightsee and maybe have dinner with the Barringtons while you're there. Let's finish breakfast. It looks fabulous, Mom. Then you can pack up. I'll make reservations."

Eliana filled her plate and joined them at the table. *But I can't leave Grandma here alone. Her stomach tightened at the thought of abandoning her in such a helpless state.*

She put on her perkiest grin and added, "I'll go check on Grandma, too, and let her know you'll be away for a few days."

"What's the rush? Why such a sudden trip?" Grace ladled more eggs onto her plate.

Eliana's eyes pleaded with Johnny to go along with the plan.

Johnny nodded. "Yeah, Mom. Doesn't that sound like fun? We need a getaway. You deserve to have some fun." He looked at Eliana for approval.

"You two. Have you been cooking this up to surprise me?"

"Finish your breakfast, Mom. I'm going to find a hotel." Eliana swiped open her phone and tapped on the screen.

"But you haven't eaten, sweetie."

Eliana lifted her biscuit and bit into it. "I'm eating. I can multitask, you know." She winked at her mom and took a nibble, swigging her coffee between bites, praying her stomach would receive it.

Johnny's phone pinged. From Sis. *We have to get out of here. Fast.*

Eliana gave him a stare that meant business.

Johnny shoved the rest of his biscuit into his mouth, then scooped his eggs on a fork ready to plunge them in. He swallowed about half of what was in his mouth and garbled, "I'll go grab a few things." He sprinted toward his bedroom.

Eliana stood, took her plate, and nodded. "Good idea, kiddo. I'll go make those reservations and you can take off right away.She followed Johnny to his room.

When Eliana entered, Johnny pushed his door closed. "What's going on?"

"I don't have time to explain, but we could all be in danger here. Do what it takes to get her out of town, and keep a low profile for a few days. I need to check on Grandma, then I'll be out too. Go. Pack a few things and smile. I don't want her to worry."

"You're worrying *me*."

Eliana hugged her baby brother and squeezed his arms. "Where did those strong muscles come from? You've grown into a fine young man. I'm proud of you. Daddy would be proud of you, too. I'm counting on you to take care of Mom."

"Now you're really scaring me."

"No. Don't be scared, just be careful. There could be some people who want to hurt you. I love you."

"Are you two conspiring again?" Grace peeked in Johnny's room.

"I'm just bragging on this handsome son of yours and giving him his marching orders."

"Ordering me around, as usual." Johnny smiled and elbowed Eliana.

"While you two pack, I'll put on my pearls and go check on Grandma. Johnny, I'll text you the reservation information. Love you both. Have a great trip." Eliana held her mom's embrace a little longer than usual and whispered, "I love you so much."

Grace held her at arms' length and peered past the pretend smile, right into her trembling heart. "Whatever is going on, sweetie, it will be okay. Look to God. Trust Him. Remember your name."

Eliana nodded and swallowed hard. With lips pressed together to restrain her emotions, she waved, and headed to her car in the back. That uneasy feeling still gnawed at her insides. She cranked the car and breathed, *Lord, I can't protect them. Please cover them with Your hand. Lead me where You want me. I need Your wisdom and direction. Show me.*

~~

After breakfast, many residents at the memory care facility played cards, exercised, or made crafts. Eliana signed in and walked past several rooms where activities brought loud laughter from the residents and caregivers. As she turned into the hallway a young man dressed in scrubs came out of her grandma's room. When he saw her, he ducked his head, spun around, and hurried in the opposite direction. *Whoever that was sure wanted to avoid me.*

Eliana quickened her steps and looked inside her grandma's room. Patricia sat in her chair, Bible to the side, cradling a small bowl of some kind of fruity pudding. Her shoulders high, she rocked back and forth in fast motion, huffing.

Eliana looked around. *They know she won't eat without help. Did he bring this? Does he even belong here?* Eliana took the bowl from her, sniffed it, and placed her beloved Bible in its proper place. Her grandma let out a sigh when her lost treasure was returned to her. A tiny smile softened the edges of her mouth. She settled into a gentle swaying motion and relaxed her shoulders.

"I'll be right back, Grandma." Eliana kissed her forehead.

Eliana looked into the hall both ways and spotted Mildred carrying some linens. "Hi, Mildred. When you finish there, would you have time to come to Miss Patricia's room for a minute?"

"Sure thing, Miss Eliana. I'll be there in two minutes."

Eliana placed the bowl in a small clear trash bag from her grandma's bathroom and tied the top to seal it. When she returned, her grandma had opened her Bible and sat as if she were listening to the most powerful sermon she ever heard. A calm countenance surrounded her. Grace and peace exuded from her every pore.

Eliana sat next to her, patted her arm, and let her heart settle. *She's okay. Mom and Johnny are okay, but Granddaddy? Sweet Granddaddy. Did Abram somehow kill him? We thought it was a heart attack when Mom found him slumped over his desk. I'll have to look at his appointment book to see if anyone came in that day.*

She gazed at the woman of God beside her, oblivious to the turmoil within Eliana. *Perhaps she has one foot here and the other is in the presence of Jesus. What a joyful transition she'll experience when she slips from here to there.*

"Grandma, I love you so much. I have felt your prayers for me these last few weeks. Thank you for praying for me all these years. God knows I've needed His presence. Your faithfulness to Him, to your family, has helped make me who I am today."

Patricia broadened her smile and bobbed her head slightly. She lifted one hand from below the Bible to the top, and patted the pages.

"Do you want me to read to you, Grandma? Here, I'll read to you if you want." Eliana gently took the Bible and held it in front of her. *1 Kings 19. Elijah again. This can't be coincidence.* "Then he came there to a cave and lodged there; and behold, the word of the LORD came to him, and He said to him, "What are you doing here, Elijah?"

Mildred came into the room with a joyful smile. "Miss Eliana. How are you? So good to see you."

"Mildred, I'm sorry to take you away from your patients."

"No problem. I'm always glad to see you and visit with my sweetheart here." She patted Patricia's shoulder. "Oh, reading about one of my favorite prophets, I see. Elijah. He was an amazing man. I love that he was so human, afraid at times, but then when God got a hold of him, boy that man could summon fire from heaven. Glory!"

"I agree. He was something. I always have plenty to learn from him."

"The Good Book is the best place for learning. I know you done been to school and have your degree and all that, but it always thrills my soul to see people learning what matters, God's Word."

"I agree. I'm afraid too many people miss out by neglecting It. I wanted to ask you about the orderlies or maybe nursing staff here. I saw a guy I didn't recognize a little while ago. Young, muscular, dark hair, blue scrubs."

"No one here wears blue scrubs. We all wear the bright floral ones, like this." Mildred held her hands to the side to showcase her colorful tunic.

Eliana nodded and picked up the bowl of dessert. "When I came in, she was holding this. Was this part of her breakfast?"

"I can't imagine why that would be here, Miss Eliana." Mildred held up the bag, shook her head, and returned it to Eliana. "No, I already fed her breakfast and she did have some good applesauce with it, but nothing like that. What is it?"

"I don't know, but I am a little concerned that a stranger came in her room and left her this."

"I am too." Mildred leaned over to study Patricia's face. "She looks okay." She felt Patricia's forehead. "Do you think she ate any of it?"

"It was just like this." Eliana lifted the bowl. "The spoon was upright, and the bowl is pretty full, so she might not have eaten any. If he didn't feed it to her, Grandma wouldn't have taken a bite by herself.

Mom, Johnny, and I are going to be out of town for a few days. Would you mind alerting the staff to keep an eye on her?"

Eliana wrote down her phone number and handed it to Mildred. "Do you have a phone that I could call or text you, so I can check on Grandma?"

Mildred called it out to her and Eliana added it to her phone contacts. "Would you mind sending me a short text every day, to let me know she is all right?"

"Be glad to, Miss Eliana."

Eliana looked around the room. Nothing was amiss, other than the bowl. "I don't like the idea of a stranger coming in or bringing her food."

"I have no idea who it was, but we can look at the security pictures if you think you might know him."

"Mildred. You're a genius. Yes, show me where I can see the security footage."

~~

Text to Johnny. *You have reservations at a Hilton Garden, near Times Square. Emailing you the confirmation number and address. Be careful. Look for anything unusual and anyone who might follow you or try to befriend you. If they say they are my friend, or anything like that, don't believe them. Grandma is fine. I'll be in touch soon.*

First stop, hospital lab. *If my high school lab-tech friend is there, she should be able to analyze or know where to send the dessert to be analyzed.*

"Anna, Hi. Great to see you." Eliana presented the bagged bowl to her friend. "I need to know if there's any chemical, any kind of drug added to this."

"Sounds sinister." She took the bowl and held it eye level to examine the contents. "Congratulations on your law school graduation. Are you doing private investigations and tracking down criminals now?"

"Kinda. Can you do the analysis here? Will it need to go somewhere?"

"I'll have to send it to the state lab and bring in toxicology and pathology, but I have a friend there. I'll expedite it and let you know."

"I suspect it will be something lethal to a dementia patient in her eighties."

"Patricia? Please tell me someone isn't trying to poison your grandma."

"That's what I want to find out. Right now, I have my suspicions, but I want to know for sure."

"I'll get it to them right away. If they find something, by law it has to be reported."

"Thanks so much. I hope it's clean but need to know for sure." Eliana wrote her phone number on a note pad, and peeled off the page. "Please, call or text me at this number with the results."

On the way back to her car, Eliana texted Julie. "Please call when convenient."

Eliana, back at her mother's house, found her granddaddy's appointment book and tabbed to February 18. *No appointments written in. He did block out a fifteen-minute slot before lunch, but it had no name beside it.*

A few minutes after ten, Julie called. "Hi. Glad to hear from you."

"Things are a little intense. Quick question. Is Matt there today?"

"Actually, he's not. He called in. Why?"

"Do you know if he was in the office February 18?"

"Hmm. Let me look back at my calendar. Sometimes I make notes about … February 18, he was out of the office that day. What's going on? Wait. I know you can't say. Promise you're being careful."

"Thanks. I promise. Gotta go. You be careful too, and of course, don't mention that you heard from me."

Eliana looked at her screenshot of the guy in scrubs. "Gotcha, Matt." *Now to dig into his family and their businesses. Somehow it ties in with Abram and the files he gave me to research.*

She packed her laptop into her satchel, along with the copies of emails she printed out and Grandaddy's appointment book, opened the back door, and nearly stumbled over a man standing there.

"Excuse me, ma'am. Sorry, didn't mean to startle you. Handy Lawn Service. I rang the front bell and no one answered."

Eliana had cross-examined enough witnesses in mock trials to spot a phony. "We don't have a lawn service."

"That's why I am here. Milton—he wanted to keep the place looking nice, and I wanted to give your mom a few months of free service to honor him. Just checking for any pets that might be in the yard on the lawn before I spray."

"Mr.—?"

"Joe. Sorry. I'm Joe. You must be Eliana. Your grandfather talked a lot about you."

"Mr. Joe, let's hold off a while on the lawn service. I appreciate the thought. But, some other time." Eliana walked around to the front of the house with him. *His truck does have lawn service emblem on the side and a tank of some sort on the back. Am I being paranoid?* "Have a good day, Joe."

"You too, Miss. Nice pearls." He winked and stepped into the truck.

Eliana's face flushed, and the hair on the back of her neck bristled. She watched him back out of the drive and creep out of the neighborhood.

When he was out of sight, she walked to the front porch and pressed the doorbell. *Works fine. What was he up to? Did he torch Julie's cabin? Was he here to set our home on fire too? Some kind of accelerant in the tank? I should have taken a picture of his truck and tag.*

She returned to the house, and sat at the kitchen table. "Lord, help me. You have shown me Elijah's life story, how he honored You while his life was in danger. What is it You want me to do? Do you want me to confront Abram like Elijah confronted Ahab?"

Her mother's Bible lay on the table. Eliana picked it up, slid it into her satchel and started out the door. This time, she glanced out the curtain before she turned the door handle.

No one in sight, Eliana made it to the car, tossed her satchel in the passenger seat, buckled her seat belt, and turned the key.

Click.

That's not good. Dead battery or sabotage? Will I activate a bomb if I try to crank it again? That's the way it happens in the gangster movies.

"*What are you doing here, Eliana?*"

"Lord?"

"*What are you doing here?*"

"Lord, I am trying to find the truth. Trying to keep my family safe."

"What are you doing here?"

Eliana realized she was acting on her fears rather than listening for direction from God. "I get it. I'm trying to do everything myself rather that trust You. Lord, forgive me. Show me how to honor You."

"Go. You will meet with Abram, Friday. He will see you and you will warn him to forsake his plan and turn to Me."

"Yes, Lord. Thank You."

Eliana breathed in a fresh breath of peace and exhaled her fears. *I asked for direction. Now I have my mission. I might be as weak as a butterfly, but God will use me.*

When she turned the key again, the engine cranked. She drove out of the neighborhood and exited onto the main highway.

After a couple of miles on the highway, a lawn service truck sat idling on the shoulder. The driver held a phone to his ear. As Eliana looked to see if she recognized his face, "Joe" turned and spotted her. He placed both hands on the steering wheel, spoke quickly into the phone, and pulled out into the traffic two cars behind Eliana.

This guy is so conspicuous. *He must believe I'm naïve enough not to see him.* A few miles down the road, he turned off, and a blue Ford Focus from behind the lawn service truck picked up her trail and stayed two cars behind her.

How obvious can they be? Where can I lose them? What's crowded on a Tuesday at lunchtime? I'll get in line at a drive-through and see what he does. Eliana made a sharp right turn when she saw the long line at Chick-fil-a. *This will work.*

Two cars back, the blue Ford followed her right turn. Eliana got into the long line surrounding the place, and the Ford pulled around to the exit side, parked in a parking space, but stayed in the car. Eliana called 911. "There is someone following me. I think I'm in danger. Could you please send someone to check out a blue Focus, parked in the Chick-fil-a parking lot, on Hwy 27? He's on the east side by the pickup window. Thank you."

When Eliana still waited for one car in front of her to pick up their order, the local police swooped in and parked in front of the Ford, blocking it. *That will keep him busy for a little while.*

Eliana smiled, saluted him with a waffle fry, and pulled out onto the highway.

I'll find a motel outside D.C. until Friday. That will give me a chance to do some research and be prepared for my meeting.

Ping. The car synced her phone to Bluetooth. "Text message from Anna." Eliana pressed "listen" on the screen.

The automated voice read, "Text from Anna, sent today at 3:15. *Barbiturates and neuromuscular relaxants. Midazolam, propofol. Euthanasia-type drugs. Enough to kill ten men. It would have appeared she died from a heart attack. Forwarding report to the authorities. Be very careful.*"

Unseen icy fingers clawed through her neck to her spine. *They tried to murder Grandma. If she had lifted the spoon to her mouth ... Matt. Abram. Cold-blooded murderers.* Her hands weakened, but she steered the car to the shoulder, opened the door, and leaned over while her stomach wretched out its contents.

She caught her breath, wiped her face, and sat up in the driver's seat. *Now I have some evidence. Thank You, Father, for protecting Grandma. Please keep Your hand over Mom and Johnny. I am trusting You to show me every step in order to do Your will.*

To Anna. "Thank you so much. Will you please text a PDF of the report to this number?"

~~

Around nightfall, Eliana found a small motel and asked for a room where she could park in the back. She explained to the kindly older man behind the desk, that she wasn't in trouble with the law, but there were some people looking for her who wanted to hurt her. *He probably hears this all the time and thinks I'm full of bologna.*

He nodded. "I've seen you before."

"I worked in D.C. for a little while and was at the University in Charlottesville before that."

"No." He shook his head and his eyebrows furrowed. "It was in a dream. The Good Lord told me you would be here, and I was to take care of you. That's what He said. You have something very important to do for Him, that is, and I am to take care of you, no matter what. That's what I'm going to do. Take care of you. Don't you worry. Me and the Good Lord, we have it all worked out."

That phrase.

Is he an angel? Is Mildred?

"Isn't that just like something the Lord would do? Thank you, sir. I prayed for God to show me what to do, and He sent me to you. I'm so thankful to meet you and know that God has put us both here."

"For such a time as this, ma'am. He's done told me you're in danger. I'll keep a lookout for you."

Eliana paid in cash and backed her car into a parking slot a few doors down from her room. Now for some rest and research. She thought about ordering pizza but wondered if her cell phone calls could be tracked. She called the desk and asked the gentleman if there was a take-out pizza place nearby.

"I just ordered some pizza and breadsticks for both of us. You need to stay out of sight, remember? I'll bring them to your door and knock twice when it comes."

'You're already blessing me, sir."

When the two knocks came, she pulled out some cash and shoved it into the gentleman's hand when he handed her the warm boxes.

"No, ma'am." He held his palm flat and pressed it back into hers. "I'm doing this for the Lord. He'll repay me. You have a good night. Call the desk if you need anything." He nodded to her and left, "There's bottled soft drinks 'bout halfway down the hall. Want me to get you some?"

"Thank you, but I will get something. Dr. Pepper in there?"

The clerk gave her a thumbs-up then added a wink and a nod that assured Eliana she would survive.

Dazed and tired, Eliana looked at the boxes and then up to the stars of the heavens. *Is there anything too great or too small for You?*

Eliana laid the pizza and breadstick boxes on top of the small refrigerator and pulled out a warm garlic breadstick and a slice of gooey pizza. *What a wonderful God.*

She rinsed her hands and pulled out a few dollars to get something to drink from the machine. With a refrigerator in the room, one trip out would be all she needed to buy enough for a few days. Eliana used her shirt to cradle the bottles to her room.

After she put them in the refrigerator, she pulled out her mom's Bible and her computer for cross references and word studies.

I'll have time to look into Matt and Abram tomorrow.

Tonight, spending time in the Word of God comes first.

Lisa Worthey Smith

Chapter Eight

Eliana booted up her computer and opened the well-worn leather-bound Bible to 1 Kings chapter 17, where the story of Elijah began. She re-read the story and replayed the dreams—or perhaps visions—of walking alongside Elijah as his story played out. Confronting Ahab, ridiculed by the people. Jezebel using her ploys to sway Ahab away from Almighty God to worship idols. The ravens, the food. She read about Obadiah and his faithfulness in the middle of a godless palace, working for a godless king.

She read about the widow God prepared for Elijah and how God resurrected her son. Eliana imagined the scene. This mother tended to her son the best she could, but despite everything she did, he became so weak he couldn't raise himself out of bed. The mother sat at his bedside and bathed his face with her tears while he lost strength, and every breath became a struggle. His eyes pleaded with her to do something, but there was nothing to do. She held his hand and sang to him.

He wheezed and coughed until he could no longer fight. His eyes fixed on the ceiling, and after a moment, his body went limp. She squeezed his hand, watched for his chest to rise, and listened for a breath. Not hearing one, she jostled his arm and begged him to breathe. Wailing his name, she pleaded with him to wake, but he didn't.

"It's Elijah's fault!" She lifted his lifeless body from his bed and carried him to the prophet. "Why did I ever deal with you, O man of God? You have come to me to bring my iniquity to remembrance and to put my son to death."

Elijah shook his head. "Give me your son." He took the boy from her arms, carried him up to the upper room where Elijah was living, and laid him on his own bed while the widow wailed in agony below them.

The prophet put his mantle over his shoulders and cried out to God. "O LORD my God, have You also brought calamity to the widow with whom I am staying, by causing her son to die?"

Three times Elijah stretched himself and his mantle over the lifeless body of the boy and wept, crying, "O LORD my God, I pray You let this child's life return to him."

The LORD heard the voice of Elijah and gave him what he prayed for. With a great gasp, the boy revived and spoke to Elijah.

Elijah wept tears of gratitude and told the boy, "Come. Show yourself to your mother." The prophet lifted his hand to help the boy rise from the bed. After he gained his footing, the boy followed Elijah down from the upper room to where his mother writhed in grief.

He spread out his arm toward the boy and told her, "See, your son is alive."

Staring at her son who had been cold and lifeless just minutes before, the woman leapt from her seat and wrapped her arms around the boy. She alternated holding him at arm's length and embracing her son. Her son who died, now lived. Her tears of hopeless despair, now tears of joyous gratitude. As it sank in that he truly lived, she clung to her son and looked at Elijah. "Now I know that you are a man of God and that the word of the LORD in your mouth is truth."

She sat and her son sat beside her. The mother stroked her son's head. "My son was dead. Now he has life again. Blessed be your God."

~~

After three years, God spoke to Elijah and told him to go before Ahab again. Eliana tried to imagine how Elijah's heart broke for the people suffering from the drought. Eliana pictured him traveling along dry creek beds, with bone-thin people—his people, God's people—sitting under shelters, bearing despondent faces of hopelessness.

Elijah's heart must have cried out, "O my people. Why did you turn from Adonai? Why did you fill your hearts with idols? Can you not see that YHWH waits for you to repent and turn to Him?"

Eliana's heart broke with Elijah's. *Father, that is my desire for Julie, for the clerks, for Justice Abram.* Eliana read on as Ahab shouted, "Obadiah! Come."

"Yes, my king." Obadiah rose from his room near Ahab's throne and sprinted toward the king. He stood in front of the throne with his head bowed, afraid his face would betray his secret about the missing bread.

"Obadiah, these years without rain or dew, have left the livestock with little to eat. Go through the land to all the springs of water and to all the valleys. Perhaps we will find grass and keep the horses and mules alive. If we do, we will not have to kill some of the cattle."

Obadiah bowed. "Yes, my king. As you wish. May I suggest, if we separate and each go through one half of the land, we will divide the time and effort to locate the water and grass."

"Agreed. Prepare for the journey and meet me here at sunrise tomorrow."

"So be it, my king."

The next day, Ahab and Obadiah set out to survey the land, each going in opposite directions alone. As Obadiah traveled, he met Elijah and stopped him. "Your mantle and leather belt—are you, a prophet? Is this you, Elijah, my master?"

"I am Elijah. Your garment tells me you are of the king's household."

"Yes, master. I am Obadiah, over the king's household."

Elijah asked, "Why do you call me master if you serve the king?"

"I only serve the king as my occupation. I am truly a servant of the Most High God, as are you. I was in the king's service the day you came to him years ago. I recognize your voice."

Elijah said, "Perhaps the wrath of God has been delayed to the house of Ahab because of you."

"I am afraid I have very little influence on the king. I did manage to hide one hundred prophets away from the queen's death orders. If the king knew, my lord, he would—"

"Thank you, Obadiah, faithful servant to God Almighty. Our LORD has indeed placed you well to serve Him. You are still young. He will no doubt use you through the coming years."

"O prophet, I pray that is true. I pray He will give me the means to show His people—our people, Israel—how to turn back to Him before it is too late."

"YHWH hears your prayers, Obadiah. One thing at a time, my friend. Trust Him and listen. He will instruct you."

Obadiah, nearly overcome with emotion, lowered his head at the word from Elijah. "He must have placed you here today, knowing I would travel this route. He sent you, knowing I was alone, to encourage me to hold fast."

Elijah responded, "And your presence encourages me. I thought I would be the sole YHWH-believer here. Why are you out here instead of taking care of the household?"

"The drought. The king's livestock have little food left. He and I are trying to locate areas with water and grass for the livestock, so they don't starve."

"Obadiah, here is your mission. Go to the king. Tell him 'come see Elijah here.'"

Obadiah's face lost its color. "What? Have you perceived that I committed some great sin, and you want me to die at the hand of Ahab? All these years the king has sought you after you told him the rain would be withheld. He has traveled in every kingdom and nation, and has required each nation to swear you were not in their realm. If I go and tell him you are here, but the Spirit of the LORD takes you somewhere else when I bring him here, he will kill me. I have obeyed the LORD from my youth, and I will continue to serve Him. I hid those prophets of the God of Abraham, Isaac, and Jacob when Jezebel set out to slaughter them all. I hid them in caves and fed them every day. I did all that in service to the LORD to be killed now?"

"Obadiah." Elijah placed his hand on Obadiah's shoulder.

The young prophet shook his head. "No, Elijah, you must listen to me. You might not know that while you were gone, Jezebel has brought in prophets of Baal, some four hundred and fifty of them, and four hundred prophets of Astarte, the Asherah. They all eat at Jezebel's table. She is dangerous."

"Obadiah," Elijah continued. "You already told me you place your loyalty in the LORD of hosts, not Ahab's or Jezebel's army or false prophets. That loyalty is well-placed. We both trust the same LORD." He waited to allow Obadiah time to absorb the truth before he continued. "You may trust my word to you because the LORD himself told me to show myself to Ahab. It will be done as He said. I will show myself to Ahab today."

Eliana imagined Obadiah's stomach knotting as he returned to face Ahab. The young prophet clenched his hands in front of him and bowed before the king. He swallowed hard to moisten his throat so the words wouldn't stick there. "I know where Elijah is, my king."

"Speak up. I can't hear you."

Obadiah cleared his throat. "It's Elijah, my king. I know where he is."

"Elijah? The filthy prophet who came before me and thinks he holds back the rain? Where has he been? We looked everywhere. I thought he must be dead."

"I promise you, my king. He is not dead. I saw him and I will tell you where he is."

Obadiah told Ahab the precise location and scurried to his room to pray.

Ahab rode on his horse to the place where Elijah waited. When Ahab saw Elijah, without dismounting, he guided his horse in a circle around Elijah as he addressed the prophet. "Is this you? Elijah? The troublemaker of Israel?"

Elijah sat still and replied. "I have not caused trouble for Israel. You have. You and your father have. You both forsook the commandments of the LORD and led Israel in following the Baals. Now I call you to gather all four hundred and fifty prophets of Baal and all four hundred prophets of the Asherah and meet me at Mount Carmel with all of Israel."

"I will summon them and meet you there."

Ahab must have thought this would be to his amusement and could be to his benefit if he could kill Elijah in the presence of many witnesses who would tell of his great destruction.

Mount Carmel. Eliana cross-referenced the topic and refreshed her memory of events there. To the west of the Dead Sea and south of Hebron, stood the mountain where another king of Israel, Saul, stacked stones in remembrance of his great victory over the exceedingly wicked Amalekites. He had obeyed God and had destroyed the Amalekites but he had not obeyed His command to also destroy every ox and sheep, camel and donkey, that their sin had also defiled. Instead, Saul not only kept the Amalekite king alive, he chose the best of the livestock to bring home with him. When he returned to Israel, Saul built the monument to himself on Mount Carmel.

The prophet Samuel had confronted Saul about the sin. "Has the LORD as much delight in burnt offerings and sacrifices as in obeying the voice of the LORD? Behold, to obey is better than sacrifice, and to heed than the fat of rams. For rebellion is as the sin of divination, and insubordination is as iniquity and idolatry. Because you have rejected the word of the LORD, He has also rejected you from being king."

Though Saul admitted his sin, the LORD took the kingdom of Israel from Saul that day.

Now, some two hundred years later, Elijah set up an opportunity for another king and the people of Israel to admit their sins and repent. As all of Israel gathered that morning, with Ahab and all the prophets of Baal and Asherah, Elijah stood and spoke to the people. "How long will you hesitate between two opinions?"

He motioned with one hand to the empty space beside him and challenged them. "If the LORD is God, follow Him."

Elijah motioned with the other hand toward the prophets of Baal and challenged them again. "If Baal, follow him."

Eliana pretended she was in the crowd. The air was thick with tension. No one moved or spoke. Ahab watched.

Elijah lowered his hands. "I alone am left a prophet of the LORD, but Baal's prophets are four hundred fifty men. Let them bring us two oxen. They will choose one ox for themselves, cut it up, place it on the wood but put no fire under it. I will prepare the other ox and lay it on the wood and I will not put fire under it.

"Then you call on the name of your god, and I will call on the name of the LORD. The god who answers by fire, He is God."

The people nodded and murmured among themselves. They agreed that Elijah had a good idea and decided they'd do as he suggested.

When they brought twin oxen, identical brothers, Elijah said to the prophets of Baal, "Choose one for yourselves and prepare it first, and call on the name of your god, but put no fire under it."

The prophets cast lots, chose an ox, and tugged on its rope to lead it to be slaughtered. They pulled and kicked at it, but the ox would not move.

Eliana found some Jewish texts of the event that indicated the ox spoke to Elijah. "I will not go willingly to be sacrificed to any god other than Elohim, my Creator."

The serpent spoke to Adam and Eve. In Eliana's previous dream, God used birds to speak to Elijah, why not an ox?

The stunned prophets stared at Elijah and the ox, and accused Elijah of somehow making his words come from the animal.

The ox refused to move. Elijah walked to the ox and placed his hand on the beast's shoulder. "I understand. But your sacrifice and that of your brother will both glorify Elohim because today He will show His power in a miraculous way."

The ox nodded and followed the men.

The prophets prepared their sacrifice and called on the name of Baal from morning until noon, "O Baal, answer us."

No voice answered; neither did any fire appear under the altar, only the searing heat from the sun.

Elijah stood with the other ox, watching with his hands on his hips.

The Baal prophets sprang up on top of the altar and cried louder to their god.

Elijah shook his head at their futile screams and sat to watch the spectacle. He pitied their blind service to an idol that would never hear them. With the hope some would see the ridiculousness of their antics, he encouraged them to cry out louder. "He may be busy or gone somewhere on vacation. He might be asleep."

They not only cried out in even louder frenzies, but through the afternoon they stabbed themselves with swords and lances until they were blood-soaked and exhausted from their efforts.

No smoke.

No fire.

No answer from any god.

Elijah stood again, and called the people to come away from the altar with the unconsumed offering to Baal, and draw near to him.

Ahab watched with his arms folded across his chest as the crowd shifted from the bloody altar to Elijah.

The prophet pointed out the dismantled altar of LORD, Adonai, which Ahab and Jezebel had ordered torn down. "This is where our people worshipped the one God, Elohim."

Elijah turned and rolled a stone into place, calling out the name of one of the twelve sons of Israel as he placed it on the spot of the dismantled altar. After he placed that stone, he carried another and again called out the name of one of the sons of Israel. He gathered and laid all twelve stones, calling out each son's name, reminding the people of their fathers. They were also descendants of Abraham, Isaac, and Jacob, to whom the word of the LORD had come, "Israel shall be your name."

When he completed the altar, Elijah dug a trench around it and reminded them, Israel, of their heritage, their God who brought them out of slavery in Egypt. He spoke of the miracles, the signs, and the wonders He brought.

The prophet arranged the wood, cut the ox in pieces, and laid them on the wood, speaking of the reasons for the sacrifice, the sins that required it, the warnings YHWH had given about neglecting His Law.

Then he turned to the people and said, "Fill four pitchers with water and pour it on the burnt offering and on the wood." Several men gathered the water and poured it over the meat and the wood.

The prophets of Baal climbed down from their altar and watched Elijah seemingly thwart his own god by dousing water over what would need to burn. They pointed and scoffed about his ridiculous "water fire."

Elijah ignored them and ordered four more pitchers of water to be poured over the altar. "YHWH, use their uncleanness for Your glory."

The Baal prophets laughed louder.

When Elijah ordered four more pitchers of water to be poured on the altar, the prophets of Baal roared and mocked the "flames of water" that soaked the altar and filled the trench around it.

At the time of the evening sacrifice, Baal's altar held the unconsumed ox and the blood of his prophets.

Elijah prayed by the altar to the LORD, "O LORD, the God of Abraham, Isaac and Israel, today let it be known that You are God in Israel and that I am Your servant and I have done all these things at Your word. Answer me, O LORD, answer me, that this people may know that You, O LORD, are God, and that You have turned their heart back again."

Fire from the LORD fell with a whoosh and consumed the burnt offering, the wood, the stones, and the dust. The consuming fire even licked up the water in the trench.

The people, astonished at the sight, fell on the ground face down and confessed, "The LORD, He is God. The LORD, He is God." They cried over their sin and transgressions to the LORD, their God.

After their confession, Elijah told the repentant crowd to get up and apprehend the prophets of Baal. "Do not let one of them escape."

The people seized the prophets and followed Elijah to the brook Kishon, where he slew the men who deceived the people. When he came back, Elijah told Ahab, "Go eat and drink, for the drought will soon end. There is the sound of the roar of a heavy shower."

~~

Ahab scratched his head and looked around. Preposterous. There had been no rain for years, and he didn't hear any roar. No clouds dotted the sky. He didn't smell rain in the air, yet he just witnessed this man—that crazy man—call down fire from the heavens. The king remembered the first time Elijah came to him. That declaration that no rain would come until …

He rose, ate and drank as if it were his own idea, now that the "entertainment" concluded.

~~

Elijah and his servant left the king and went up to the top of Carmel and found a solitary place to pray. There, the prophet of God crouched and lowering his face between his knees, praising Almighty God for all He had done. Praising Him for showing Himself to the people so they repented.

He said to his servant, "Go look toward the sea."

The servant went up and looked and came back to report, "There is nothing."

Elijah continued his intercession for the people and praise to El Elyon for His presence, His power over all the elements, and his provision of the storehouses of rain. He asked his servant to go again and look toward the sea.

The servant obeyed and came back with the same response. "Nothing."

Elijah told him seven times to go back.

The seventh time his servant returned and said, "There is a cloud—a small cloud, about the size of a man's hand—coming up from the sea."

Elijah's heart quickened and his blood coursed through his veins with such purpose his limbs tingled. "Go. Tell Ahab 'Prepare your chariot and leave, so the heavy shower does not stop you.'"

~~

Ahab tilted his head and drew his eyebrows together at the "suggestion" from Elijah's servant. How dare he order the king. He lightly brushed the crumbs from his clothing, stepped into his chariot, and nodded to the driver to begin the journey home. This man had already done the impossible today. It might be prudent to listen now.

The clouds came into sight and Ahab's heart must have sunk as he thought about the defeat of the prophets who sat at his wife's table all these years. The words Elijah spoke about the God of Abraham, Isaac, and Jacob rang true.

The wind swirled up dust into his eyes, but he could see the clouds growing dark. He urged the driver to hasten, but the heavy shower overtook them. *Rain*. As Elijah had said. Rain. First the altar, the fire, now the rain. *What did Ahab think of this man?*

He reached out his hand to feel the cool refreshing rain. As they neared the palace in Jezreel, where Jezebel stayed most of the time, they passed by the temple of Baal. A glorious temple. Jezebel was so pleased with it. Surely Ahab wondered, "What will I tell her? She will be furious to hear her prophets have been killed. Elijah may be crazy. He may be powerful. But he'd better beware of her fury."

~~

Eliana's scene shifted to follow Elijah. With the hand of the LORD on him, Elijah outran Ahab's chariot to Jezreel. People stood outside their homes, hands lifted to let the rain run down their elbows. They pulled out every pot they had to gather the precious rainwater they missed for years. Those who went to Carmel told of the alter, the fire, and Elijah. Some shook their heads in disbelief. Others remembered the tales from their fathers about the mighty hand of God.

~~

When Ahab arrived at the palace, he peeled his dripping outer garment off as his wife came to greet him.

"See, my king." She held out one arm for him to see the henna tattoos swirled over her skin. While he put aside his cloak, she brought the other arm to the front and waggled a bouquet of fragrant lilies under his nose. She broke off one and placed it behind her ear to hold back her hair and tucked the rest into her sash. Wrapping her arms around his neck, she whispered, "I have sought Baal and Astarte today. Do you smell the jasmine in my hair? Now, my king, the gods have heard and brought you rain."

Ahab shook his head. "You don't understand."

"What do I not understand?" She dropped her arms to her side. "You know I have pleaded to the gods and brought offerings to them." She lifted her skirt and pulled up one leg to expose the henna swirls on her foot. She flashed him a quick glimpse of the henna tendrils on her calf and thigh before lowering her leg to the floor. "My king, it is raining as I requested. What do I not understand?"

"Your prophets." Ahab hung his head, trying to find a way to explain it all.

Jezebel drooped her shoulder and leaned her head on his chest, encircling his waist with her arms. "Yes, my king. Yes, my love. Yes, to your every desire—"

"Jezebel." He pushed her by the shoulders to arms-length away from him and let out a heavy sigh. "Elijah's God and your prophets." He swallowed hard and started again. "I'm telling you the prophets of Baal could do nothing. They tried, but Elijah's God proved more powerful today."

Jezebel shook her head and pursed her lips into a pout. "No."

Ahab pushed down on her shoulders. "Sit, my queen. I have more to tell you."

The queen sat heavily in the lush chair and fingered the fringe on her sash. As he told her the events of the day, her face reddened. She wadded the sash into wrinkled knots as her eyes darted around the room searching for someone to scream at, something to throw.

Ahab sat beside her and wrapped one arm around her shoulders. "My love. He killed them."

"All of them."

Jezebel shook free from his embrace and sprang to her feet. She jerked the flowers from her waist, threw them across the room, and glared at her husband. Her eyes filled with rage. Through clenched jaws she growled, "He will die. I will see to it he will die!"

She lifted up her skirt so her feet would not be entangled, and stormed out in search of a servant to do her bidding.

~~

Obadiah heard the commotion and started toward the king's room. Before he reached there, Jezebel had stopped a young man in the hall. Obadiah flattened himself in a dark corner, watched, and listened.

Hands on hips the queen half growled, half shouted her venomous orders to the wide-eyed youngster, "You. Go find this Elijah. I don't care what it takes. I don't care what you have to do. Give him this message from me. Warn that filthy little man that as he killed the prophets of Baal, so may the gods kill me if I don't make his life tomorrow as theirs is today. Now go. Find him. Tell him." She pointed to the door and screeched, "Go."

The trembling youth bowed before his queen, then turned and ran out into the rain. Jezebel held up her hands and shrieked with all her breath into the rain of the night.

Obadiah huddled in his room, looked up toward heaven, and prayed for Elijah, for himself, and for the messenger.

~~

Eliana pictured the events. The young man pounded on the door-frame where Elijah stayed. "I'm the messenger of Jezebel and I am here to see Elijah."

Breathless, the palace servant described the scene he just left and the raging urgency of the queen to kill him. "I've never seen her like this, Elijah. She means to kill you. If she knew where you were, she would have killed you tonight, but be assured, the queen will send out all the military to find you and have you killed tomorrow. Ahab will not stop her. She is probably giving her instructions to them now."

"You did well, young man. Go back and tell her you did as she requested. God be with you." Poor fellow. He'd likely face punishment no matter what he told the raging queen.

Elijah's servant saw the man out and then returned to his master. "We must go, Elijah. We need to leave now." His chest heaved. He wrung his hands. "Master, we must leave this place before we're killed."

"You are right." He gathered his mantle and strapped his belt around his waist. "Let's go. Now."

The eager servant grabbed his cloak and followed his master out into the dark. The sounds of the rain hid any noise from their steps as they left the city. They crouched low and held their cloaks over their heads when they passed windows. Inside, families were rejoicing about the rain and the crops that would benefit from it.

Once outside the city, they ran for their lives south, toward Judah. All through the night, they sprinted as quickly as they could through the muddy trails, deep into Judah's wilderness. In the early morning just before sunrise, they came to Beersheba, towards Edom.

Weary in mind and body, Elijah found a secluded place for the two of them to sit unnoticed. The prophet formulated a plan, and it did not include this innocent man.

"My faithful servant, the time has come for us to part ways."

"Master, what have I done to displease you?"

"Nothing. You have served me well. I have done as the LORD asked of me, but now my life is finished. You heard the palace servant. Jezebel will not stop until she finds me and kills me. It will be better for you to be away from me when that happens. We'll rest here for a little while, but after the women have brought their water from the wells and the men have gone to the fields, I will go from here into the desert, alone."

The servant pressed against his stomach to quiet its rumbling. Elijah smiled. "You are hungry. So am I. Go get some food, and find another job. You'll be fine."

The two sat together until the townspeople were inside and quiet. When no one was on the street, Elijah stood, placed his hand on his servant's shoulder, and said, "Goodbye, my friend. God be with you."

Chapter Nine

Eliana sighed at his exhaustion. Powerful people were out to kill him, people were in danger because of him, yet, God's mission still remained to be done. *Lord, is this why You told my mother You would use me like Elijah?*

The story continued as Elijah and his servant parted ways. After the previous day of exhilaration and running, the prophet's heavy legs stumbled, protesting the demands he'd made on them. He stopped in a brushy place far outside of town, pressed his hand against the muscle that screamed for relief in his side, and lifted his chest to expand his lung capacity.

He turned and scanned the open area behind him for any sign of pursuers while his side cramp eased and lungs claimed the air they desperately needed. The dust his feet had stirred settled back onto the earth. No bushes or grasses rustled along the path, except where a pair of doves waddled around the edge searching for grain.

His knees buckled under him and he recruited his hands to pull his weak body under a juniper bush, thick with yellow blossoms. Elijah leaned back on its thick trunk and allowed his throbbing leg muscles to rest. He inhaled the thick fragrance the plant released when he brushed against the flowers. The sweet scent of the blooms brought a calm into his chest. He breathed in and out with deliberate steadiness.

"They are coming—" He paused to capture another breath. "—to kill me." He gazed at the cloudless sky and waited for YHWH to respond. His eyes pleaded for a sign, a word. Nothing.

After all the years of service, the obedience, the prayers answered, surely, he had done enough. What human could do more? "YHWH, You know I am here. You know I am finished. Take my life. I've given all I can."

Elijah turned his trembling palms up and lifted their emptiness in an offering to Almighty God. The fullness of his life had already been given. He raised his hands higher toward the vast blue sky. "No human could do more. Just let me die here rather than at their hands. Please."

The doves cooed and fluttered off, and Elijah lowered his hands to the dirt. He held his breath while his eyes searched along the path for intruders, murderers.

He waited. Listened.

Only stillness answered.

Assured he was alone and out of sight, he looked back to the sky. No word or sign from heaven came in answer to his plea.

He coughed some of the dust from his throat, pulled his mantle from his shoulders and used it to wipe some of the grit from his face. Elijah fingered the thick, hairy cloak that had rested on his shoulder these many years. The LORD was with him. That alone brought peace to his weary soul.

Sliding back onto the welcoming branches of the bush, his legs relaxed. The prophet stretched out to lie on the soft dirt under the tree and allowed the fragrance to soothe his exhausted, troubled spirit.

Hopeful these would be his last moments on earth, his body collapsed in surrender to the fatigue. He muttered, "the beasts will have their meal after I breathe my last."

"Get up." A strong voice and a tapping on his shoulder startled him from the fog of his sleep. "Get up" the man repeated.

His heart pounded within his chest and he tried in vain to force his dry throat to swallow. I've been found!

Elijah blinked hard to clear his eyes and pressed his elbows into the sandy dirt beneath him, prepared to die by the sword. No strength came to his limbs, but his vision sharpened. The man who stood before him bore no weapon. Rather, he held out his hands toward Elijah with a gift, a cake of bread.

"Get up and eat." The man leaned toward Elijah and placed the loaf near his head. The aroma of the bread enticed the prophet to inspect the gift from this stranger. Gathering himself into an upright position, he reached out, picked up the warm loaf, and pulled off a piece of the crust.

With two fingers, he placed a morsel in his mouth while he scrutinized the man before him. His imposing stature and muscular build suggested he might be a warrior, but his face reflected more compassion than aggression. A few small bites of the hearty bread gave unexpected satisfaction to his hunger and peace to his heart.

Is this a dream? Is this an angel of the Lord who has come to me? Has YHWH heard my plea and sent this messenger? Has my spirit departed or is it about to be taken?

God opened Elijah's eyes to recognize the truth that he indeed entertained a heavenly messenger. The gift bearer motioned to a jar of cool water he had placed alongside Elijah.

Eyes locked on the angel, Elijah lifted the jar to his mouth and let the clean, cool water rinse down the bread and refresh his parched throat. Mesmerized by the presence of this man, he ate and drank in slow motion, but his mind raced.

Why is he feeding me instead of taking me? If I have left my earthly body, why has he not taken me to the presence of the LORD? Before he could ask any questions, in one blink the angel vanished.

Elijah finished the loaf alone and licked the crumbs from his hands. Heat can cause delusions. Did he imagine the angel, the bread?

I bet it was even better than the pizza and garlic sticks I ate.

He glanced at the earthen jar beside him, patted it, and smiled. It was real. An angel did bring it. Elijah lifted it to his mouth again. The contents quenched the deep thirst within him. The LORD was still with him. He would not die of hunger today.

If this angel gave him food, he might also give him protection from his enemies. Elijah lay back under the tree while his heart settled and his body and mind demanded rest. Satisfied, he drifted to sleep for the evening.

A second time Elijah awoke to find the angel standing beside him with his hand on his arm. Again, he told the prophet, "Get up. Eat." This time he added, "The journey ahead of you will require great strength."

The prophet rose up, ate another cake of fresh bread, and drank the cleanest water that had ever passed his lips.

The angel had said "the journey ahead." *I can't stay here. I have to go.* He pushed up with his arms, now refreshed and strong, and saw a two-peaked mountain to the south. Mount Sinai and Mount Horeb, the mount of God where Moses received the tablets. Where he struck the rock and YHWH provided water. If any place was safe, it was there.

Elijah shook out his mantle, twirled it over his head so it landed around his shoulders again, and set out in the strength of the food brought to him by the angel.

The roads grew dustier and more desolate the farther he went from town. For forty long days and nights, he alternated between sprinting and walking toward the mountain. If he spotted anyone on the road, he hurried off to the side and hid among the scrubby bushes.

He often praised God for the heavenly food given to him by the angel. Like no earthly food, it sustained him for the days, now weeks, he had been traveling. Not even a hunger pang rumbled within him.

With his sprint/walk pattern, Elijah had now distanced himself from suspicious eyes, though he still looked around for any rising cloud of dust that indicated Ahab's horsemen following his trail.

Eagles soared above and cast their shadows over him as they circled in the heavens, releasing a whistle now and then. Lizards, nearly invisible until they moved, made his heart skip a beat.

Assured he was alone, Elijah plodded now. One step, then another in the searing heat. He thought of the refreshing rain Elohim sent on the dry and barren land. He prayed the rains brought life to the land and to the people, and that they recognized the rain came from Almighty God, the one true God.

Elijah thought of his servant and prayed he remained safe. He wondered about the widow and her son. He prayed they remembered that the Most High God raised the boy from the dead and provided many miraculous meals for all of them during those many days. Step after step, he replayed his life and prayed YHWH counted it as good.

When he reached the mountain, he climbed to a hollowed-out area where he could hide and rest. He spread out his mantle and rested in the dark shadows deep within the rocky shelf.

Elijah would have been able to look out over the mountain where Moses and the children of Israel waited for the LORD to direct them, to give them His Law. He probably remembered the glory of the LORD appeared on the mountaintop above them like a consuming fire after Moses had been up there many days. He would have pictured the people waiting below, who had witnessed so many miracles, grumbling and doubting, falling back into the ways they learned in Egypt and making the golden calf.

Just days before, the LORD displayed His glory to that generation of the people of Israel. He consumed the sacrifice with fire from heaven. He withheld, then released the rain. Would the people, His chosen people, return to idol worship as their fathers did in the time of Moses? Even after the rain? Or would Jezebel take credit for that and continue to spread the worship of Baal? "O, Jehovah, God of Abraham, Isaac, and Jacob, I pray You press into their hearts to remember You alone are God Almighty. Adonai, turn this generation of stubborn and rebellious people to You forever."

Amen, Elijah. Amen. I pray that with you for this generation before me today.

While he was praying, the word of the LORD came to him. "What are you doing here, Elijah?"

This is the passage I read for Grandma. This is what God asked me. The words might have hit Elijah hard like they did me. He wasn't "doing." He was hiding, although he thought he had done his job.

I let my fears have priority instead of listening to what God wanted me to do. I tried to handle everything on my own.

Elijah responded with an explanation. "I have been working zealously for the LORD, for the LORD of hosts, Jehovah Sabaoth. The sons of Israel have forsaken Your covenant. They have torn down Your altars and killed Your prophets with the sword." He hung his head and shrugged his shoulders. "I alone am left. They are looking for me now, to kill me too."

Me too, Elijah.

Eliana read more. "The word of the LORD spoke to Elijah again. 'In the morning, go stand on the mountain before the LORD.'"

He rested in the cool of the cave that night. When the warmth of the morning sunlight touched his head, Elijah woke and came out to the mouth of the cave. He sensed the LORD was passing by.

A strong wind bashed the mountains and whistled through the cracks and edges of the stones. Elijah pulled his mantle securely around him as mighty rocks broke into pieces and fell around him, but the LORD was not in the wind.

After the wind settled, he heard a deep rumble and felt the earth tremble under his feet. As he tried to maintain his balance, the earth groaned and shifted around him, but the LORD was not in the earthquake.

After the earth stilled, a fire appeared. It reminded him of the fire that consumed the sacrifice only days before. A fire so glorious … but the LORD was not in the flames, and the fire vanished.

After the fire, a silence fell over all the mountain, engulfing Elijah with peace. Within the silence blew a gentle wind. Elijah wrapped his face in his mantle and stepped out into the breeze, and inhaled its tranquility.

A voice came to him and said, "What are you doing here, Elijah?"

Eliana again understood Elijah's thoughts. "I don't understand. You see me and know my heart. You have seen me stand against Ahab and Jezebel and their Baal prophets. I am here because she vowed to kill me. Is the mountain of God not the best place to be? What can I do but wait to die?"

Elijah explained again, "I have been very zealous for the LORD, Jehovah Sabaoth, the God of hosts; for the sons of Israel have forsaken Your covenant, torn down Your altars, and killed Your prophets with the sword. I alone am left; and they seek my life to take it away."

The LORD said to him, "Go, be on your way and return to the wilderness of Damascus. When you have arrived, you will anoint Hazael king over Aram. You will anoint Jehu, the son of Nimshi, the king over Israel. You will anoint Elisha, the son of Shaphat of Abel-meholah, as prophet in your place. It will be that the one who escapes from the sword of Hazael, Jehu will put to death. The one who escapes from the sword of Jehu, Elisha will put to death. Yet I will leave seven thousand in Israel, who have neither bowed their knees to Baal nor have their mouths kissed him."

Elijah bowed low before the LORD, wept, and repented from his arrogance. How could I have doubted the power of Almighty God? He sends and withholds rain, wind, and fire. He directs even the unclean birds to steal from Ahab's table. Why did I fear Jezebel's wrath more than the LORD of Hosts?

I am no different from the rebellious children who stood here generations ago. Why did I give up? Why did I not seek His counsel on what to do? Why did I hide?

How did I not know that thousands were in Israel who did not worship Baal? How could I have thought I was the only one?

Almighty God, forgive my doubtful and prideful heart. Let my remaining days be fully and wholly dedicated to serving You, no matter the obstacles that seem overwhelming. May I be faithful to show Elisha Your ways, that he may serve You better than I.

Eliana climbed down from the bed, and knelt. *Oh, Father. You asked me what I was doing. I am here because You brought me, and prepared this place for me with someone who will care for me as the widow cared for Elijah. Thank You.*

Thank You for not giving up on me.

Forgive me for asking You for direction so many times but acting before I stopped to listen for Your answer and direction. My mind and heart became consumed with fear for my family and heartache over my granddaddy.

Forgive me for thinking about vengeance that belongs only to You. Forgive me for fearing Abram and Matt more than looking to You.

I know You hear me. I am listening now. Show me and equip me for what you want me to do Friday. I pray as You instructed us, in Your name. Amen.

Eliana wept in release of those fears and in submission to His will.

She climbed onto the bed, pulled out her mother's Bible, and opened it to the Old Testament. Deuteronomy 20, verses three and four were highlighted in yellow. "He shall say to them, 'Hear, O Israel, you are approaching the battle against your enemies today. Do not be fainthearted. Do not be afraid, or panic, or tremble before them, for the LORD your God is the one who goes with you, to fight for you against your enemies, to save you."

Fighting enemies, facing them without fear or panic. Eliana breathed in the perfect balm for her frayed nerves.

She flipped a few pages and the Bible opened to 2 Samuel 22 and read verses three and four, highlighted in yellow. "My God, my rock, in whom I take refuge, my shield and the horn of my salvation, my stronghold and my refuge; my savior, You save me from violence. I call upon the LORD, who is worthy to be praised, and I am saved from my enemies."

'Enemies' again, but my God will save me from them. Oh, Lord, thank You.

Psalm 138, verse seven in yellow. "Though I walk in the midst of trouble, You will revive me; You will stretch forth Your hand against the wrath of my enemies, and Your right hand will save me."

Oh, Father, my enemies are coming against me, but You are far more powerful. Eliana's eyes teared.

She turned to the New Testament. The Bible fell open to 2 Corinthians, and her eyes focused on a section of chapter 4 highlighted in yellow. "… we are afflicted in every way, but not crushed; perplexed, but not despairing; persecuted, but not forsaken; struck down, but not destroyed."

She soaked in the wonderful promise there and gathered a sense of the intensity of the battle she might encounter. Eliana flipped a few pages and opened to Hebrews 13. Her mother had highlighted verses six and seven. "—so that we confidently say, 'the lord is my helper, I will not be afraid. What will man do to me?'" Remember those who led you, who spoke the word of God to you; and considering the result of their conduct, imitate their faith."

Mom, Daddy, Grandma, and Granddaddy. Their faith has strengthened me so much through the years, and now, right when I need it so much. She reached up to finger the pearls. *I need to check with Mildred.*

To Mildred. *How's the patient today?*

Ping. *A little tired. Sleeping a lot.*

Should I be worried?

Ping. *Her and the Good Lord got it all worked out, I'm sure. Don't you worry.*

Love you, Mildred. You are a blessing to us all.

Ping. *Love you too, honey.*

Eliana returned to the Bible and turned a few more pages to a bookmark in Ephesians. The bookmark had her name on one side. "Eliana" My God Answered. On the other side, "Elijah" My God is YHWH. Opening to chapter six, Eliana again spotted a passage highlighted. She read verses ten through seventeen, marked in yellow. "Finally, be strong in the Lord and in the strength of His might. Put on the full armor of God, so that you will be able to stand firm against the schemes of the devil. For our struggle is not against flesh and blood, but against the rulers, against the powers, against the world forces of this darkness, against the spiritual forces of wickedness in the heavenly places. Therefore, take up the full armor of God, so that you will be able to resist in the evil day, and having done everything, to stand firm. Stand firm therefore, having girded your loins with truth, and having put on the breastplate of righteousness, and having shod your feet with the preparation of the gospel of peace; in addition to all, taking up the shield of faith with which you will be able to extinguish all the flaming arrows of the evil one. And take the helmet of salvation, and the sword of the Spirit, which is the word of God."

She rested her head on her pillow and soaked in the words—the truths God showed her—dispelling every fear and equipping her with faith and courage. *No matter what the rest of the week holds, Lord, I will trust You.*

Her mind soothed. Every fear faded into the background. *I asked for guidance, and when I took time to listen, God provided what I needed for the task. Thank You. My God answered.*

Chapter Ten

Wednesday morning

Two knocks at her door woke Eliana.

"Breakfast," a man's voice announced from the other side of the door.

"Thank you." Eliana replied.

Eliana opened the door and found a bag of sausage biscuits.

The clerk was a few doors down the walkway. He turned and waved.

Eliana called out another "Thank you." *He is feeding the sheep, as Jesus asked Peter to do. Like God asked the widow to do for Elijah. What a blessing to know He is looking out for me.*

Still filled with peace and comfort from her time in the Word of God and with God, she basked in the joy of it all. *God created me for a purpose. He told my mother about it before I was born. He has woven all these events to come together intending to use me. Eliana. Small-town Eliana, just out of law school, and God put me in front of a Supreme Court justice to remind him of God, with an even bigger meeting coming up.*

She sat cross-legged on the bed, unwrapped a warm biscuit, and took a bite of the buttery, savory goodness. While she relished the delightful breakfast, she picked up her phone and checked her text messages.

From Johnny. *Mom and I are ok. Sight-seeing today. Nice hotel. Checking with grandparents to see when they might want to get together.*

Good. All is well.

From Mildred. *Miss Patricia is fine. Someone came to ask about her, but didn't go to the room.*

Thank You, Lord.

She plugged in the coffee maker and opened a cellophane package with coffee grounds and a filter, poured in the water, and pressed start. While it gurgled to life, she opened her laptop and logged in to the hotel wi-fi.

What do I need to know about Matt and his family? Their profiles and resumes are stellar. What are they hiding?

All morning, she searched for information about Matt's father. She discovered pictures of him with a wealthy European businessman who was often in the news funding "anti-fascist" groups from racial to religious.

He tossed around "fascism" as if the US had been replaced with a dictator. The open-market, freedom-loving United States where the people elect their leader, fascist? Who would believe such nonsense? Those who don't know the truth. Those who sit under professors who spit out opinions instead of factual history. The young people who are roused into a frenzy and topple statues that remind them of the past.

This businessman had already toppled a few small countries' economic systems, and aided non-citizens to infiltrate and vote against any God-fearing candidate. He's had groups working on government-issued and funded debit cards, and ways to eliminate American currency. One article claimed his power on Wall Street went beyond his stock holdings to blackmail secrets he held over certain large firms. *Including the firm where Grandfather Barrington worked.*

He has been there a long time, Eliana thought, and is a vice president of something. Would my grandfather know anything about this? His "anything to make a dollar" motto and lack of religion would make him susceptible, even if he didn't know the big picture. That could be why the Barringtons never accepted us. I always thought he was disappointed that Daddy never aspired to be a rich, big-city lawyer. His wife, my grandmother, never had a loving relationship with anyone or anything except money and the prestige that came with it. If it brought in money and power, the Barringtons would be all for it.

The foundation's leader is mentioned in legislation about decriminalizing everything from marijuana to illegal entry into the United States. On the other hand, he stood for criminalizing Bibles, Christian churches, prayer, even military and police presence. He funneled millions into election campaigns that suited his purpose, and to lobbyists to lavish on congressmen to sway them toward more centralized government control. *Exactly what he said he hated, fascism.*

The name of this same businessman, Matt's father's friend, popped up as funding for Marxist groups in countries steeped in Communism, and many pro-Muslim groups and Muslim candidates for office.

Interesting. Then again, both Marxists and Muslims are obligated to destroy the Christians, so he could use them for to accomplish that purpose.

Ping. From Julie. *Emma is very sick. Todd is at the cabin, taking care of insurance. Pray, please.*

Eliana phoned Julie. "Hi. I'm so sorry to hear about Emma. What can I do to help?"

"I'm scared." Julie sniffed. "Really scared. She spiked a fever during the night, and this morning she wouldn't wake up. The doctor admitted her to the hospital, and now they are talking about putting her on a ventilator."

"Is anyone with you?"

"No," Julie whimpered.

"Would you mind if I come to just be there for you?"

"We're in the children's wing. Third floor."

"I'll be there as soon as I can."

God, direct the doctors taking care of Emma and help Julie see You, and come to know You. Show me how to minister to them.

~~

Julie sat crumpled in an ICU waiting room chair, head buried in her hands.

Eliana sat next to her and put her arm around Julie's trembling shoulders. "Julie, I'm here."

Julie turned and embraced Eliana. "God is punishing me for—"

Eliana pressed against Julie's shoulders to unlock the hug and bring the two face-to-face. "God loves you. He loves Emma."

Julie kept her head down as tears flowed. "How could He love me when I have killed my own child? Why would He love me after that? How could He forgive me for that?"

"No one has done enough good things for God to love them, and no one has done enough bad things that He could not love them. If you heard of Paul, in the Bible, you might know he killed Christians, but that didn't stop God from loving him. God made Himself known to Paul, and taught him, then used him to teach many, many people about God. Paul ended up writing much of the New Testament. After our phone call, that's what I prayed for you."

Julie raised her head. "You prayed for me?"

"I asked God to direct the doctors taking care of Emma, then I prayed that God would help you to see Him, so you would come to know Him."

Julie shook her head. "I don't know what to say."

"You don't have to say anything."

"No. I mean, after we talked, I was sitting right here, and I heard a voice, but I was alone. I don't know. It was weird."

"Tell me."

"I felt a rush of something surround me, like stepping into a warm shower. Peace and security flooded over me. Then I heard a man's voice call my name. It was someone I knew, but I didn't recognize the voice. Like I said, weird. I looked around the room, and no one was here. It made me wonder if God had spoken to me. I had no idea you were praying for me. Maybe I did expect it; after all, you have prayed for us before. I just have so much going through my head right now."

"I'm here." She patted Julie's arm. "But more importantly, God is here. He can supply a peace that goes beyond comprehension. He wants to."

"That's a good description of how I felt. I went from turmoil to calm when I heard my name spoken."

"Julie." Eliana squeezed her hand. "That's what God is like. He wants to give you peace. He wants you to look to Him and trust Him, no matter what."

"If I do that, will He heal Emma?" Julie's eyes pleaded.

"I don't know. This isn't a bargaining tool for Emma's life or health. This is about forgiveness, so you can have peace here and then eternal life with Him when you leave this life."

Julie nodded. "What I heard was real. I want what you have. I want that kind of calm and wisdom, regardless of the circumstance. I don't deserve it, but I want to know God."

"Would you like for us to pray about it now?"

Julie nodded and wiped her tears. Eliana grasped both Julie's hands and prayed. "God, You are so good. You are so faithful to Your Word. Thank You for calling to Julie today. You have promised to love us and forgive us of our sins if we admit them to you. Lord, Julie wants to know You, wants You to be part of her life. Fill her heart with Your Holy Spirit so she will walk in Your ways."

"Julie, if you want to know Him, this is your time to talk to Him. You can pray something like this 'I know I am a sinner. I need Your forgiveness. I believe You are God and that Jesus is Your only Son. I believe Jesus died for my sins and was raised from the dead. I want You to be the Lord of my life from this point forward, and I ask it in Jesus' name.'"

Julie closed her eyes and breathed out a sigh. "God, I don't remember everything Eliana said, but I do know I heard You today. I have fought against You all my life. I have not listened when You told me the right way to go and I did what I wanted instead. I have sinned so many times. Please forgive me. I see now that You are God, whether I admitted it before or not. I believe Jesus died for my sins. Will You forgive me? I want to give You my life, from this day forward. In Jesus' name, amen."

Eliana folded her new sister in Christ in her arms and they wept together.

"I feel like a weight has lifted from my shoulders. What do I do now? What about Emma? What about Todd? I want them to know too."

"It is God's will that everyone comes to know Him, so it's okay to pray for that, like we just did."

"But I guess I can't tack on a prayer for a million dollars, can I?" Julie joked.

"It's good to see that smile again. No. Always pray for His will to be done. When Jesus faced death, He asked if there was a way to avoid the suffering he would endure on the cross but added that He wanted God's will more than His own desire to avoid the pain. 'Not my will, but Thine be done.' That's where His peace comes in, trusting His will, no matter what happens."

A nurse came into the waiting room. "You're Emma's mother, right?"

Julie stood. "Yes. May I go see her now?"

The nurse came toward her and sat in a chair alongside Julie and asked her to sit. She looked at Eliana. "Is this a family member?"

"She's my friend. It's okay for her to hear whatever you have to say."

"Is your husband back yet?"

"No, it will be another hour or more, depending on traffic."

The nurse pressed her lips between her teeth and shook her head. "I'm sorry. We don't have that much time."

Chapter Eleven

Julie stared at the nurse, then grabbed Eliana's hand.

The nurse swallowed hard, grimaced, and spoke in a soft, compassionate tone. "The doctor needs to intubate Emma right away. If you want to talk to her, you may go in now. I don't promise she will be able to answer, but she won't be able to talk after we intubate."

"Are you saying she is dying?"

"No." She hesitated and took a breath. "I wouldn't say she is actively dying. Her condition has worsened, but we're doing everything we can. The doctor wanted you to have a chance to talk with her before she's intubated, if you want to." She stood and waited for Julie's answer.

"Can my friend come with me?"

"Yes. You can't stay long, though."

Julie gripped Eliana's hand, and they followed the nurse around the corner into the Pediatric Intensive Care Unit.

Emma's frail body lay limp on the bed, surrounded by beeping machines. Her intermittent rise of her chest showed her struggle to get a good breath, even with the oxygen mask covering her nose and mouth.

Julie released Eliana's hand and sat next to her daughter. She stroked a stray hair away from her face and kissed her perspiring forehead. "Hi, sweetheart. It's Mommy. I'm here, Emma. I love you."

Emma lifted one eyelid and whispered something.

The nurse lifted the mask slightly, revealing the girl's pale, bluish lips. "Try again, Emma. Tell your mommy one more time."

Emma's lips curled into a smile. "Mommy."

"I'm here, darling. Mommy is right here."

"Mommy, Jesus loves me."

"You're right, sweetheart. He does."

"He told me. I saw my brother. Jesus loves him too."

Tears flooded Eliana's face. *Thank you, Father.* She covered her mouth to stifle her sobs from interrupting this God moment.

Julie nodded. "I know, baby girl. I will see him one day too."

"Yes, Mommy. Jesus told me you talked to Him, and we'll all live there together one day." Emma's voice faded, her eyes rolled back, and a machine beeped furiously.

The nurse pulled on Julie's arm. "You need to go now and let us intubate her."

A mechanical voice called out "Code Blue PICU" from a speaker in the unit. Attendants rushed into the room. "Code Blue PICU."

"I can't leave her," Julie pleaded and tugged against the nurse.

"Code Blue PICU."

"Let us take care of her, please." The nurse pulled her away from the bed. "You'll only be in the way here."

"Code Blue PICU."

"It will be better for Emma if you wait in the waiting room." The nurse barked instructions to the attendants who answered the code blue. She turned back to Julie. "I'll give you an update as soon as I can. I promise."

Eliana locked her arm in Julie's and ushered her toward the waiting room. Julie slouched in a chair and Eliana sat beside her.

Julie sat, her face lowered and propped up on her elbows. "God, I know You are here. I feel Your presence. Be with my precious Emma. Don't let her go through this alone. Be with Todd. Help him arrive here quickly. Help him understand. Help him see You."

The minute hand dragged around the face of the waiting room clock. Eliana prayed fervently for Julie and her new found faith, for the doctors to have wisdom.

For Emma.

For Todd.

Ping. From Johnny. *Met with grandparents today. Grandfather Barrington offered to send me to Harvard, where Dad and Granddaddy went to, and he offered to get me in with his agency on Wall Street. He showed me around. Pretty impressive place. Amazing opportunity. Exciting. Grandmother Barrington took us shopping. Mom wants to go back home and check on Grandma.*

Ping. From Mildred. *Miss Patricia not doing too good today.*"

Julie's phone rang. "I'm sorry, Your Honor. I'm at the hospital with Emma … No. I'm not. I can't leave her … I do, sir, but I can't leave my little girl. Hello?" Julie stared at her silent phone.

Todd stormed in, spouting obscenities. "What is going on?"

Julie stood and raised her hands to embrace Todd.

He billowed into defense mode, pulled his arms up through hers, and thrust them to the side. "Don't put your hands on me. What happened? Where's Emma?"

"Try to be calm, Todd."

"I am not calm, and I have no intention of being calm until I see my daughter." He stomped around the room. "Where is my little girl?" His face reddened, and his volume increased with every phrase.

Eliana stepped toward him. "I'm Eliana, Julie's friend from work. Emma is in the PICU and the doctors are working with her. She's had trouble breathing and they were intubating her a few minutes ago."

"Where's her doctor? I want to see her doctor now." He marched toward the door. Julie grabbed his arm from behind. Without turning around, Todd elbowed her to the ground and jerked open the door, screaming profanities, "I am going to see her doctor right now."

In moments, security rushed to the scene and tried to restrain him. Julie leaned against the door, tears spilling down her cheeks. She lifted her palms toward heaven and said, "God. He needs Your help. Please help him."

Todd took a deep breath and shook off the security guards. He raised his hands to signal surrender. "I'm sorry." His voice broke. "I just want to see my little girl. That's all. I don't mean anyone any harm. I just … want to see … my baby girl."

The doctor came around the corner. "Julie? Oh, good. Todd. I'm glad to see you're here. Let's step into a private consultation room."

Todd put his hands on his hips. "No. Just tell me here and now. How's my little girl and when can I see her?"

The doctor shoved his hands into the pockets of his white coat and began with a quiet voice, "When we first saw her a couple of weeks ago with the respiratory virus, we treated her for that. She responded to treatment, but today, as you know, she spiked a fever. It seems the virus came back with a vengeance. Her chest x-ray today shows significant fluid in and around her lungs, and also around her heart. You know her lungs and heart were both underdeveloped at birth, which resulted in mental and physical limitations." His eyes darted between the anguished parents. "We are doing all we can, but you need to be prepared to make some decisions about quality of life. I'm very sorry." His beeper sounded and he rushed back out toward the PICU.

Julie and Todd stared at each other–powerless to help their daughter in the fight of her life. The blood drained from their blank faces. They stood in silence while the doctor's words echoed in the room, stabbing their hearts.

Todd reached out, tenderly took Julie's hand, and led her to the chairs. They sat side by side without a word. The bustle of the hospital faded into a deafening silence while they waited.

Tears dripped from Julie's stoic eyes.

Todd's foot tapped the floor and he swallowed his sobs.

Eliana never felt more helpless as she counted each heartbeat hammering her temple.

About thirty minutes later, the somber doctor shuffled back into the waiting room. He took a breath and lowered his head. "I'm very sorry. We did all we could. Her heart simply couldn't take the strain. She has no brain activity. We left her on the ventilator so you can say good-bye. A chaplain is on the way. If you will come with me." He motioned to the door.

Julie and Todd plodded hand in hand out of the waiting room.

Eliana clutched her writhing stomach and whispered, "Dear God, You promised my mother. You promised me that You would use me as You did Elijah. She named me Eliana, 'My God Answered,' and I believe that You do. When the widow's son died, You raised him at Elijah's request, so that they would know You. Father, I am asking

You to do the same here. Restore Emma's heartbeat. Restore her lungs. Restore her brain activity. Do what the doctors can't and raise her, so that You will be glorified and they will know You are God. I pray as fervently and as full of faith as I know how. I will praise You whether You choose to raise her or not. I pray only for that which is according to Your will, and in Jesus' name. Amen."

Eliana rocked back and forth in her seat in the waiting room, but with every passing minute, her mind tried to prepare her heart to be shattered. *What will I say to them?*

Thirty minutes later, Julie opened the door. "You're not going to believe this." Julie's grin told Eliana there was miraculous news.

"Try me." Eliana beamed, and chill bumps fluttered up her arms.

Julie told her about Emma's cold hands and lifeless body. "While we were in the room with Emma, I talked to Todd about God. We prayed together for God's will to be done with our little girl. Then, while we were praying, Emma squeezed my hand ever so slightly. Eliana, she opened her eyes and talked to us."

Tears and laughter finished out the story of God's grace and the flabbergasted medical staff. "She's going to be fine. Just fine. I don't know how to thank you."

Eliana's heart rallied with praise. "Thank God. Thank God Almighty." She clapped her hands in praise, then unclasped her pearls, and handed them to Julie.

"I want you to have these. They are the pearls my grandma wore on her wedding day, the start of her married life. The pearls are a reminder of all the prayers she offered for me and how I needed to live up to them. I want you to have them on the day you start your new life with Christ. Wear them as a reminder of how God heard and answered our prayers. Today is the beginning of a journey with the Lord. I will pray for you on this journey that you will grow deeper in your faith as days go by."

Julie cupped the pearls in her hands. "I don't know what to say. It's such a precious gift. I shouldn't accept them."

Eliana wrapped her hands around Julie's and squeezed them. "That's what God's extravagant love is all about. Just receiving a gift in faith."

Lisa Worthey Smith

Chapter Twelve

Wednesday night at the motel

To Johnny. *You need to keep Mom there through the weekend. See if you can get tickets to a play or something. It's important.*

To Mildred. *Thank you for the update. I can't come right now. I know Grandma and the Good Lord have it all worked out.*

Ping. From Johnny. *Can you see me as a Wall Street exec?*

To Johnny. *That's a stretch right now, kiddo.*

Ping. From Johnny. *Very funny. Mom's real worried about Grandma.*

To Johnny. *Grandma is at peace about leaving here to be with Granddaddy and the Lord.*

Ping. From Johnny. *But Mom, she's lost so much.*

To Johnny. *But she also knows what she has. Enjoy your time together. Promise me you won't make any commitments about the Wall Street offer yet.*

Ping. From Johnny. *Why? He already has me lined up. College. Everything. It's all set. We'll have it made.*

To Johnny. *I can't explain now. We'll talk later. Deeper water than it appears.*

Ping. From Johnny. *Grandfather Barrington said it would be big money, and he'd pay for college. I can swim, remember?"*

To Johnny. *Not with concrete shoes and sharks. Please. I'm serious. I have a big meeting tomorrow and I don't know how it will work out. No matter what happens, I love you. Take care of Mom. Remember who you are. I would appreciate your prayers tomorrow afternoon."*

Ping. From Johnny. *You're scaring me again.*

To Johnny. *Not trying to scare you. Just need your prayers.*

Ping. From Johnny. *When can we talk?*

To Johnny. *"Soon, I hope. I love you.*

Ping. From Johnny. *You 2, Sis."*

~~

Thursday morning

Ping. From Julie. *Thank you again for all you did for me and my family yesterday. Todd and I talked with the chaplain here at the hospital and he told us how to join a Bible study program at a church nearby.*

To Julie. *I am so thankful, so happy for you.*

To Julie. *Are you going back to work today?*

Ping. From Julie. *I'm going. Wearing my pearls. I don't know if Abram has filled my job yet. He wasn't happy with me yesterday. Right now, if it's God's will to move me somewhere else, I'm okay with that.*

To Julie. *I need to meet with him tomorrow. Will you check and see when his last appointment of the day is?*

Ping. From Julie. *Are you sure you want to do that?*

To Julie. *Yes. As sure as I've ever been about anything in my life.*

Two knocks at her door followed by a "breakfast" announcement.

Eliana replied, "Thank you." Another bag of fresh sausage biscuits sat outside her door. Eliana picked it up and waved to the clerk as he strolled back to his desk.

She pulled out a handwritten note attached to the inside of the bag. "In case somebody is watching or listening, I wrote this in a note. After you came back last night, a guy pulled in behind you. He didn't ask for a room. I noticed him on the security camera. He checked all around your car. I don't know if he messed with it but thought you should know."

I didn't even think to watch for anyone following me. If they knew I was at Julie's cabin, they probably saw me at the hospital and followed me here. Great.

"Dear Father, I have trusted You long enough not to fear men. I am trusting You to see me through this mission. You told me to go, take Your Word, and meet with Abram on Friday. You assured me he will see me, and I will warn him to forsake his plan and turn to You. Until You tell me otherwise, that's what I plan to do."

Eliana unwrapped a biscuit and pulled out her laptop to start her research. How did Matt and his family fit in?

His father, after four terms as secretary of state in Georgia, now enjoyed a private practice as a criminal defense attorney. His name popped up in newspaper articles along with pictures of him with his family in his homes on both coasts, as well as several vacation getaways in exotic locales, which fit with the income of a criminal defense lawyer who represents wealthy clients.

Eliana scrolled through more pictures of Matt's father smiling with mafia family members after he defended them at trial, and the jury found them not guilty. *Bingo.*

His sister's state representative position was up for reelection. Nothing terribly sinister there. She searched on.

Matt's sister in D.C. worked on the presidential campaign of a candidate who had strong anti-Christian sentiments. He encouraged schools to integrate Muslim teachings into the curriculum and never hesitated to scoff at American founding fathers. She now headed the legal department for the Social Justice and Equalization Foundation in D.C.

Okay. Sounds vaguely familiar. What does the Social Justice and Equalization Foundation do? The tagline on their website read, "A non-profit organization assisting marginalized people groups and causes that better humanity."

Eliana found a discussion thread about the foundation. They funded lobbyists and political candidates who support socialized medicine including abortion on demand, unlimited birth control available in schools, encouraged fair treatment of staff and students in schools regardless of sexual orientation, and promoted STD screening in schools. They were also proponents of mandatory attendance in public schools beginning at age four, and promoted the elimination of religious schools. The foundation had labs set up to manufacture mandatory free vaccinations including free euthanasia drugs for those with a diagnosis of a debilitating, incurable, or expensive-to-cure disease. The drugs would be made available with a prescription.

Euthanasia labs already in place.

Another thread spoke of the benefits of open borders, unregulated immigration, and offered funds to any candidate who might promote that. They encourage nationalization of industries, and redistribution of wealth, elimination of currency to be replaced with government-issued credit cards. An open call to pay for any video footage of Christians, police, military, or churches. An open call to pay for distributing hate-filled messages and scheduling riots. An open call to be a paid protestor for any events about shootings or Christian "propaganda."

They want to take all power from the people, disarm them, establish Socialism, and eliminate those who disagree. They wouldn't need gas chambers with enough euthanasia drugs available.

How is Abram involved?

Markham's satchel. She represents the foundation. No wonder he balked at my opinions about the sermon case and dismissed the information about Muslims.

This must be what he talked to Granddaddy about. Abram hired me for special research just to see if Granddaddy told me anything about it.

Matt's family is deeply entrenched with this. No wonder he feels untouchable. No doubt the sister seeking the congressional seat is part of the agenda too.

Markham's satchel. Did she do more than entice Abram to a particular vote? Did she deliver the euthanasia drugs for Matt's visit to Grandma? He could have used that on Grandaddy too.

God, I need You to show me what I need to know. Show me what You want me to know and what You want me to tell Abram.

Her eyes diverted to a stack of Milton's papers. *What did I miss?* She picked up his calendar and flipped back several months. Reading through short notes, Eliana noticed Thursdays and Fridays were the typical days he blocked out time for a call with Abram. Very few notations about the content of the call other than topics similar to those Abram had her research.

The day before he died, he did note a call. *Was that the same date as the email?* Eliana shuffled through the stack to find the printed copies.

Yes. The same day as the email in which Granddaddy warned Abram that he would report him to the authorities, he scribbled a note *2384, 2385.*

That's not the last four of a phone number or extension I remember. Not Granddaddy's or Abram's. Wouldn't be Matt's. All the clerks' extensions began with "3."

Legal Code? If he were to report Abram, that might be his note about a legal code. A quick search found 18 U.S. Code § 2384, § 2385.

Seditious conspiracy § 2384.

"If two or more persons in any State or Territory, or in any place subject to the jurisdiction of the United States, conspire to overthrow, put down, or to destroy by force the Government of the United States, or to levy war against them, or to oppose by force the authority thereof, or by force to prevent, hinder, or delay the execution of any law of the United States, or by force to seize, take, or possess any property of the United States contrary to the authority thereof, they shall each be fined or imprisoned not more than 20 years, or both."

Advocating overthrow of Government § 2385.

"Whoever knowingly or willfully advocates, abets, advises, or teaches the duty, necessity, desirability, or propriety of overthrowing or destroying the government of the United

States or the government of any State, Territory, District or Possession thereof, or the government of any political subdivision therein, by force or violence, or by the assassination of any officer of any such government; or

Whoever, with intent to cause the overthrow or destruction of any such government, prints, publishes, edits, issues, circulates, sells, distributes, or publicly displays any written or printed matter advocating, advising, or teaching the duty, necessity, desirability, or propriety of overthrowing or destroying any government in the United States by force or violence, or attempts to do so; or

Whoever organizes or helps or attempts to organize any society, group, or assembly of persons who teach, advocate, or encourage the overthrow or destruction of any such government by force or violence; or becomes or is a member of, or affiliates with, any such society, group, or assembly of persons, knowing the purposes thereof—

Shall be fined under this title or imprisoned not more than 20 years, ...or both, ..."

~~

Eliana leaned back against the headboard of the bed. *These people want to take the place of God, and rule the world.* "World domination." *Sounds like a conspiracy theory, but here it is in black and white. And Abram is about to implement it.*

He had to eliminate Granddaddy before he revealed it.

Now, he's afraid I know and he's out to eliminate me too.

Ping. From Julie. *He's free after two o'clock tomorrow.*

To Julie. *Tell him I want to meet him at 2:00 on the west side, by the main entrance to the court.*

Ping. From Julie. *He agreed.*

Ping. From Julie. *Please be careful. He noticed my pearls today. Matt commented on them, too. They know we are in touch. I don't like the way they talk about you. I really don't like the way he smiled about meeting you.*

To Julie. *My God Answered. That's who I am. My name means "My God Answered."*

Ping. From Julie. *That's something I never knew I could trust, until now. Emma should come home Friday evening. She's doing great. She told me about her brother, in heaven. I can't wait to tell you about it.*

Chapter Thirteen

Friday morning

Two knocks. "Thank you," Eliana called out, but no breakfast announcement followed.

Eliana looked through the peephole in the door. Shally stood outside her door. Eliana opened it and Shally hurried in, and pushed the door closed behind her.

"What are you doing here?"

Shally put her hand on her hip and began, "You and I never really had a chance to get acquainted. I'm sorry about the way we harassed you at lunch and all."

"So, you tracked me down to apologize?"

"Well, yeah. I just wanted you to know none of us dislike you or anything."

"Thank you, Shally. I'll sleep better tonight."

Shally sat on the bed and reached behind a pillow with one hand, trying to look inconspicuous. "You're not going to report us or anything, are you? I mean it was all in fun. Just breaking in the newbie. You know how that goes. We were just trying to teach you the ropes, so you would fit in."

Eliana nodded. "Although I could report several things from that office. But at this point, I don't plan to turn you in for anything."

"Are you are still planning to meet Abram tomorrow?"

So, that's what this is about. "Yes, I do plan to meet him, at two on the front steps, but obviously you already knew that."

"Good. He already has you cleared to go through security at the plaza."

"Anything else I should know?"

"No, that's all." Shally stood.

"Just how deep are you in this thing, Shally? Do you have any idea?"

Shally put a finger to her lips and pointed behind the bed.

Eliana nodded, then continued. "Do you have any idea what the weather will be like tomorrow at two o'clock. Should I bring an umbrella?" Eliana pointed two fingers, mimicking a gun.

Shally stared at Eliana with sad eyes. "That might not be a bad idea."

"Thank you, I appreciate the visit."

Shally mouthed, "I'm sorry."

Eliana nodded. "Bye. Have a good day. Give my regards to Matt and the gang."

Shally's eyes bulged and her mouth dropped. She shook her head violently and crossed her hands in front of her signaling, "no."

Eliana smiled and mouthed, "It's okay," and opened the door. The clerk stood outside and handed Eliana her breakfast.

"Good morning, sir. Thank you."

Shally hurried down the hallway.

The hotel clerk waited until she was out of hearing range. "You okay, ma'am? Everything all right here?"

"Yes, I'm fine. Thank you. I'll come down to check out in a little while. You've been very kind to me and a great blessing. Oh, would you mind calling a cab to take me into D.C. at one-thirty? And I'll need a tow truck to carry off this car."

"Something wrong with the car, ma'am? Do you want it towed to your home or to a dealership for repair?"

Eliana tore off a piece of the biscuit bag and wrote on it while she talked. "I need a new car. Think I'll tow it to a dealership and trade it in while I'm here. I'll call a cab for my errands in town."

She handed him the scribbled note. "Can't talk here. Explain later. Tampering a possibility. Towing to PD. Thanks."

He read the note silently and nodded. "I see, ma'am. I'll call one and have them get in touch with you when they arrive."

"Thank you again."

Within thirty minutes a tow-truck driver knocked at her door. She removed the car key from her key ring and gave it to the driver. When they were in the parking lot by the car, she explained that it might have been tampered with, but she didn't know how. "It might even be a bomb." She warned against cranking it and asked that it be taken to the police department with her contact information.

Around ten, she packed up her things and announced for any listening ears that she was getting an early start for her meeting, so she'd have time for a leisurely lunch.

I hope I'm wrong about any sabotage to the car. There was the unexpected dessert for Grandma, but they should leave her alone now that they know where I am. To think of working in the office with the people who did that, who probably killed Granddaddy. Lord, help me through this day.

She passed one hundred dollars in cash to the clerk with a note about where he would find a listening device in her room. "Thank you for all you've done for me. I pray the Lord will bless you and keep you, and make His face to shine upon you. I pray He lifts His countenance to you and gives you peace."

"God bless you, ma'am. Today and all your days."

"Where can a girl get a burger within walking distance?"

"The next block. See the sign?"

Eliana nodded. "Are you still going to be able to call a cab here for me by one-thirty?"

"Yes, ma'am."

"Great." Eliana lifted her satchel. "May I put this behind the desk and pick it up then?"

"Absolutely." He pulled it behind the desk.

Eliana sat in the diner and watched at least three cars circle the motel and come back out looking both ways up and down the highway.

Ping. From Johnny. *Sis. U ok?*

To Johnny. *Yes. You?*

Ping. From Johnny. *We're fine. Thinking a lot about our conv yesterday. I love you, sis. I always looked up to you. You're my hero, in case I never told you. I'll always take care of Mom. I even prayed for you. Haven't done that in a while. Thanks for the reminder. Love u.*"

To Johnny. *I needed those prayers and am counting on them today. I'm proud of you. Love you.*

At twenty after one, she walked back to the motel, gathered her satchel, and waited for her cab under the pull-through area by the doors. The driver offered to load her satchel in the trunk, but she kept it by her side and her purse in her lap.

The cab driver dropped her off just before two at the security checkpoint on the west side of the Supreme Court building. Eliana showed the guard her driver's license to confirm her identification and told him of her appointment time.

He ushered her through an X-ray while someone opened her purse and satchel. Then he pulled the note from Abram's office with her name printed on it and attached it to a lanyard for her to wear around her neck.

"Would you mind holding the satchel and my purse here? I have a short meeting with Justice Abram and I'll be right back. But Julie, from Abram's office will be coming by to pick up the satchel."

"Yes, Miss Barrington. I know her. I'll watch for her."

"Thank you."

Eliana looked at the impressive white columned building. *Temple of the law. How sad that some who sit here to judge the law only do so to increase their power.*

Eliana strode toward the gleaming building, so rich with history. On the opposite side of the building, the eastern façade bore the motto, "Justice, the Guardian of Liberty." On this western side, "Equal Justice Under Law" greeted the public.

Father, only through Your liberty and justice are we truly free. Let it be known today. Use me as You will, that people will see You and come to know You.

Forty-four marble steps led up to two bronze doors. The thirteen ton, seventeen-foot high and nine-and-a-half-foot wide doors stood as reminders of the grandeur and importance of the proceedings that took place behind them.

When Eliana was about halfway up the steps, the doors rumbled slightly as they slid to the side into pockets in the wall. Abram and Matt paraded through the opening and out onto the marbled porch. When they saw Eliana, they hesitated and looked at each other.

"Gentlemen." Eliana climbed the last few steps. "You look surprised to see me. This is the date and time of the meeting, isn't it?"

"Of course, Eliana. Good to see you." Abram scowled at Matt, and then turned back to Eliana. "How was your drive into the city?"

"I had a sudden urge to call a cab instead of driving my car, so I could enjoy the scenery. It was a lovely ride."

Abram slapped Matt on the back. "We're glad to see you, Eliana. Tell me, what brings you here? Why did you call this meeting?"

"I thought it appropriate to meet here. In this place of equal justice under the law—the place where justice will guard our liberty— some of us still appreciate our God-given liberties."

"Young lady," Abram huffed as he turned and pulled the bronze doors closed, exposing the four panels carved into each door. "Do you see any evidence of God on this door?"

He pointed to the bottom panel on the left door. "The Shield of Achilles, from Homer's *Iliad*. Two men bring a dispute before the elders who will each pass judgement. The elder with the fairest verdict will be awarded the two coins on the pedestal, and his verdict is adopted by the whole body. No god there." He waited for Eliana's response.

Eliana crossed her arms in front of her. "Lovely carving."

He pointed to the panel directly above it. "The Praetor's Edict. A Roman praetor publishes his edict proclaiming the validity of judge-made or common law. On the right is a soldier, who may represent the power of government to enforce the common law. No god there." His volume increased with every assertion of "no god."

Pointing to the panel above that Abram continued, "Julian, one of the most prominent law teachers in Ancient Rome, instructs a pupil, about the development of law by scholar and advocate, not by any god."

The top panel on that door. "The publishing of the Corpus Juris by order of the Roman Emperor in the sixth century AD. No god."

Abram shifted to the right door and motioned to the bottom panel. "King John of England is coerced by the barons, not your god, to place his seal upon the Magna Carta in 1215."

The panel above that, "King Edward I watching as his chancellor publishes the Statute of Westminster in 1275, the greatest single legal reform in our history."

The next panel. "England's Lord Chief Justice Coke bars King James I from the "King's Court," making the court, by law, independent of the executive branch of government. No god there, either."

The top panel. "Chief Justice John Marshall and Associate Justice Joseph Story discussing the 1803 *Marbury v. Madison* opinion in front of the U.S. Capitol."

Matt smirked at each reference to the lack of God and watched Eliana's face.

As if he were making his closing statement to a jury, Abram turned to Eliana and raised his arms. "Where, young lady, do you get the idea that God has any influence over anything that happens here?"

"You already mentioned Him. May I ask you what you meant by the term 'AD'? Anno Domini, perhaps?"

"It's a generic Latin term."

"No, sir, it's actually pretty specific. 'The year of the Lord.' And it references Christ, the Son of God. Have you forgotten the carving of Moses on the North wall?"

"Yes, Moses is pictured there." Abram's lips curled into a smug smile. "Along with Muhammad. Did you notice that the tablets Moses holds only list the last five Commandments that have nothing to do with your god? Do you remember that Muhammad also holds a so-called holy book, the Qur'an?"

Abram continued. "If you carry the foolish notion that the carvings here represent any obligation to God, then you must also consider all the carvings here: Aesop's fabled tortoise and the hare, Confucius, the Roman Law, the Egyptian ankh, the owl, the Justinian code, the sword of the crusader, and many other mythical items. Are they all gods?"

Abram tossed up his hands with a dramatic flourish to make his point. "There are a variety of mythological entities out there to which people have sought counsel through the years. Where are they now? They all vanished. Not one is here. Not one. Eliana, you are a bright young lady. Why do you still hold to the ridiculous notion that any of your liberties are given to you by anyone other than our government?"

Eliana opened her arms to motion wide, "Mostly because God created the entire universe and He rules it. It's His. He established the world by His wisdom, and by His understanding He stretched out the heavens. He causes the clouds to ascend from the end of the earth. He makes lightning for the rain. He brings the wind from His storehouses. All these things speak to the sovereignty of God."

She pointed to the door. "Chief Justice John Marshall, whose image you just pointed out on the door, the longest serving chief justice, knew that. He said it should be no question how to judge if the legislature violated any laws of God. He said the greatest scourge an angry heaven ever inflicted upon an ungrateful and sinning people was an ignorant, a corrupt, or a dependent judiciary."

Abram crossed his arms, rolled his eyes, and shook his head while she continued.

"In the 1600s, the first charter of Virginia recognizes the 'providence of Almighty God, and sets out to tend to the glory of his divine majesty, in propagating of Christian religion to such people, who as yet live in darkness and miserable ignorance of the true knowledge and worship of God.'"

The justice's eyes glazed over, and he stared at the door handle.

Eliana ignored him. "In 1777, the constitution of Vermont recognized individuals have natural rights, and the other blessings which the Author of existence has bestowed upon man. The Author of existence, Justice Abram, is Almighty God, not you. Most, if not all state constitutions have a phrase invoking the favor and guidance of Almighty God. The public servants, including you, all swear an oath to obey, 'so help me, God.' Did you forget your oath? Have you forgotten to seek help from Almighty God?"

A tic in Abram's jaw pulled at his cheek at regular intervals.

She continued, "Why the push to eliminate references to God from our schools? Why the push to eliminate chaplains in the military? Why the push against prayer to Almighty God? Why the delay in minting coins and the urge to eliminate currency? Justice Abram, perhaps you have heard of a foundation, the Social Justice and Equalization Foundation."

Abram raised one eyebrow and looked down his nose at her. "Justice and equalization, dear Eliana, are basic desires of all mankind.

We all want to have the same as everyone else. Didn't you realize that?"

"I realize that is the same tactic Hitler, Stalin, Mao, and Castro all used to trick people into establishing a dictatorship. These people who the foundation funds and trains in other countries—is that who the foundation for Social Justice and Equalization is shipping across our borders? Are they going to be part of the anarchy?"

Blotches formed on his neck.

"This foundation that propagandizes the rich to be the source of all the ills in the country. I suppose their solution would be to nationalize all our farms? Factories? All businesses? They must want the economic system to crumble."

He opened his mouth, but she continued. "I suppose when they ridiculed—no, they vilified—belief in God, they purposely intended that generations of young people would no longer hear the truth about their Creator and not learn about Christ. Without any responsibility to honor God's laws, they could determine their own right and wrong. That would remove any moral conscience and allow people to sacrifice their unborn children, rather than take responsibility for them. That would certainly eliminate 'In God We Trust.' I suppose you would change it to 'In the government we trust,' or perhaps 'In Justice Abram we trust.' I hate to break this to you, but you haven't earned my trust."

Abram scowled after every sentence. Eliana's impassioned speech grew louder and drew more listeners on the steps and in the courtyard.

"Is that why the foundation recruited and paid people to bait police officers and film the encounter? Is that why they used social media to post certain portions of those videos so it looked like all police were the enemy? What if they incited the people to disobey the laws and paid a bounty for every officer they killed? Would law and order cease to exist?"

"Would this high and mighty Social Justice and Equalization Foundation stoop so low as to recruit and pay violent criminals to riot in cities and loot business? Yes. They already did, and you know that. What if those neighborhoods and whole cities could not defend themselves against the looters? Would local then state governments topple?"

The justice, noting the crowd forming, flinched and loosened his collar.

"So, when the economic system crumbles, our currency becomes worthless, and when the citizens run out of coins, the government would need to provide for us, right? They might have to supply us government-funded debit cards. Of course, they would have to establish a database of citizens who cooperate and those who don't. Our phones and social media would be a good place to monitor that wouldn't it? But then the foundation already has the banking system and that ongoing list of dissenters. Right? So, when they issue the debit cards, it will be easy to limit or eliminate funding the debit cards for people who speak against the new way. Those who cooperate, who submit, who follow blindly to what the foundation has told them will have fully funded cards. How long will that last? When will they bring out the euthanasia option?"

"That's quite enough, Miss—"

"What if the rules of law and order no longer applied and so many local governments fell that the military had to step in? Let me think. Oh, yes. They have a plan for that too. That type of anarchy would require martial law under the control of, not the president, not the legislature, but the Supreme Court. It would be a revolution, with a new government, new leadership, and plenty of well-trained men and women to take the helm of the revolution. Oh, and suppose a single Supreme Court justice just happened to have an agreement in place with the majority of the justices on the bench to abdicate leaving him as sole dictator, or should we say, King Abram?"

The crowd inched closer to them and Abram interrupted her. "Eliana, dear, let's go inside." He reached for her arm to pull her to the door.

Eliana turned to evade his arm. "No, sir. Let's stay out here. It seems other people might be interested in how the foundation is manipulating them." Eliana pointed to the gathering coming up the steps.

"You have no proof. Just silly conspiracy notions of a young, misguided girl."

"Actually, I do have proof. Julie is going to pick up a few documents I've pulled together over the last few days from the guards—ah, there she is."

They all turned and shifted their focus to the guard building. Eliana waved to Julie, standing outside the guard's office. Julie returned the wave. When Eliana turned back to face the courtroom doors, a yellow butterfly landed on the bronze doors.

It looks just like the one ...

Abram snorted. "You're not a poker player, are you? You're bluffing. You have no evidence."

"How do you think I know so many details? I have plenty of evidence and so did Granddaddy. Do legal codes §18 2384 and 2385 come to mind? They seem to apply here."

Matt furrowed his eyebrows.

Eliana turned to Matt. "You might not remember off-hand. I'll remind you. Seditious conspiracy and conspiracy to overthrow the government."

The color drained from his face, and he glanced to Abram.

The justice turned toward the bronze doors. "I'm going inside. If you want to continue this ridiculous conversation, I suggest you come with me."

"Not without permission from God, you won't."

The butterfly stayed on the door.

Abram smirked. "I will. And if I want it, I'll have your head on a platter like your John the Baptist—," he snapped his fingers, "—just like that."

"Yes, you are quite skilled in that category, aren't you? My granddaddy learned that even your friends aren't exempt from your death sentences. As you said, you don't tolerate threats. So, we have another convenient death of someone who threatened you and the foundation. You didn't bother making that one look like a suicide. When we exhume his body what level of euthanasic drugs will we find? How convenient that Markham's satchel can deliver such helpful pharmaceuticals to eliminate obstacles."

Matt shoved his hands into his designer pockets and scanned the gathering crowd. Sweat beads formed on his upper lip.

Abram leaned toward Eliana and spoke in low tones, "Every war has casualties. Your grandfather was my friend. He didn't suffer." The justice then took a prideful pose as if he were the all-powerful pharaoh in front of Moses. He projected his voice to the listeners gathering on the steps and in the plaza. "Everything I've done and will do is always in the best interest of the people whom I serve."

Abram lifted his hands to the group below him. "I am a justice of the Supreme Court of the United States of America." He smiled as more assembled to watch the spectacle play out. Then he lowered his hands and voice. "I do not need the permission of your mythical god for anything I do."

Eliana locked her gaze on him. "Except open the bronze doors."

Abram laughed out loud to the people. "This foolish girl thinks I can't open the doors. I've opened them hundreds of times."

The butterfly opened and closed its wings while perched on the door. Eliana's heart pumped mettle into every cell of her body, and the Holy Spirit filled her with peace that surpassed all understanding.

She lifted her chin, "Maybe so, but you can't open them today without permission from my God. He opens and closes doors. What He opens, no man can close. What He closes, no man can open. Unless and until Almighty God—the Creator of all that exists—allows you to open the door, take me in, and kill me, as you killed my granddaddy, you, Justice, will not be able to do it."

Abram scowled and seethed through clenched jaws, "Lower your voice, young lady. You don't want me to bring slander charges against you."

Eliana shrugged. "That would only hold water if I spoke a lie. You and I both know I spoke the truth. I'm curious. What do you think the police will find when they examine my car? Hope there aren't any incriminating fingerprints or DNA."

"Doesn't matter what they find. I am king here." He pulled at the doors to slide them back into the wall, but they didn't budge. He pulled harder, grunting with each attempt.

Eliana put her hands on her hips and smiled. "We're waiting, King Abram."

After a few moments, she added, "Sir, perhaps the attendant locked it from the inside. You might try knocking and asking for help."

Abram leaned to the side to apply as much leverage as he could to slide the door, but it stood firm. He glared at Eliana and knocked on the door. "Is anyone there?"

From inside the court, a young man's voice answered, "I'm here, Your Honor."

Abram smiled and cocked his head at Eliana.

The attendant continued. "But I can't seem to open the door. I don't know what's holding it back."

Eliana smiled and raised her eyebrows in response.

"Well, get someone to open the door. Now," Abram snapped. His tone and unintended volume brought snickers from the growing audience.

Eliana offered, "Why don't you try asking someone on the door panel to help you, or from one of the carvings—Confucius, Muhammad—maybe one of them could help."

"You stupid, dimwitted moron," Abram muttered while wiping the sweat from his brow. His eyes narrowed and turned as black as his heart.

After he pulled on the door again, he changed the subject. "How's your precious little Grandmother Moore doing today? Patricia, isn't that right?"

He swatted at the flies buzzing around his sweaty face. "How's her appetite for fruit pudding these days? Oh, and how are your mother and Johnny enjoying their New York trip? Harvard and a position in a certain Wall Street trading firm will be perfect for him, don't you agree? We could use another Barrington on Wall Street."

"What I think is—for all your perceived power, you can't even open a door without permission from God, the Almighty Ruler of heaven and earth—the God who made you and Who sits in judgment of everyone. Even you, Justice Abram, will kneel before Him one day. You have a choice to humble yourself before Him now or be humbled at the judgment where you will be punished for eternity."

"Shut up." The vein on his temple pulsed. "Open this door, right now, or I will—"

"If God allows you to open the door, you will what?"

Abram released the door, whipped around to face Eliana, then whispered, "Open the door and we will go in and discuss this."

The butterfly took flight from the door. "Okay, Justice Abram. Open the door. Just don't pull too hard. Don't want to damage them." Eliana waved one arm to usher him in.

Abram pulled with two fingers, and the door slid into the wall pocket. Matt pushed the other door to the side. A flustered attendant inside straightened his cap and moved back to his station.

Eliana led them in. "Shall we?"

Matt followed Eliana into the courtroom. Abram waved and smiled to the crowd on the steps, then he winked at the guard and told him he was dismissed for the day. He pulled his handkerchief from his pocket, wiped his brow, and smoothed his suit.

"That was quite a show you put on. You show courage and promise and could be a great asset to the organization you think you know so much about. Why not join us? Be a part of a new and better government? Why not join the winning side of history?"

"Justice, if you want to be on the winning side of history, you need to abandon this whole scheme, as Granddaddy told you."

"Now why would I forfeit all I've worked for because of some temporary glitch in the doors? The world needs someone who will look out for them, someone who will provide for everyone, and eliminate all suffering. They need someone real, not a Santa Claus or a genie in a bottle they can pray to and hope will answer. They need a ruler. You see the news. People don't have the intellect to govern themselves or cast responsible votes. Look at the poverty, the disease, the hatred and the rampant violence. They can't govern themselves. The foundation will eliminate that. It's been underway for some time. Now, it is time to bring it to fruition."

Eliana pitied the man. *He is so blinded.*

Abram gloated, "Milton couldn't stop it and there's nothing you can do to stop it either." He made eye contact with Matt and motioned him toward Eliana. "Milton Moore was brilliant. I'll give him that. But he had no vision. He couldn't see the better way. Moore could have been a part of something glorious, and you all could have had anything you wanted. But he was too shortsighted, too stuck in the old ways, too immersed in his Judeo-Christian ideals to see how the world could be so much better. I'm sorry you've also chosen that antiquated rubbish."

"What if Granddaddy were right and you are wrong? What if there is a God, and He alone establishes kings and rulers."

"Then why did his God let me kill Milton? Where was He then? Where is He now?" He nodded to Matt, and the clerk wrapped his brawny arm around Eliana's neck, but the chokehold didn't take.

Abram seethed, "Kill her, you imbecile."

"Sir, I can't." Matt grunted as he wrestled against something unseen. "There's some kind of barrier. I can't touch her."

Eliana stood unphased before Abram while Matt strained, trying but unable to strangle her. "You killed my granddaddy and you will be judged for that. Right now, my guess is that God has sent an angel to restrain Matt. God had one angel kill 185,000 Assyrians in one night. One angel can certainly restrain your clerk with no problem."

"But, Justice Abram, even if He removes the angel and allows you to kill me here today, Julie is taking all the documents, all the information to the FBI as we speak. A copy has already been emailed to the president, and every member of Congress. This would be a good time to confess your sins, sir."

Matt lowered his hands, exasperated.

Eliana turned to Abram's perspiring cohort. "You and your family are deep into this. It will be hard for you to extract yourself, but you must. I know what you have done. The police have a picture of you in blue scrubs and the lab analysis of the fruit pudding you delivered to my grandma. Did you realize you were handling enough drugs to kill ten men? Time to turn yourself in to the authorities. Time to admit you need God instead of all these useless power games. Even so, you'll never practice another day of law in your life."

Matt swiped his brow, and his cheeks flamed. He swallowed hard and shifted his weight from one foot to the other.

Eliana darted from Abram to Matt. "I want you to know I am not doing this out of any spite but because God has asked me to extend to you His love and forgiveness. You must give up this plan. We all need God, including both of you, whether you realize it or not. You will never defeat Him or overpower Him. He will not share His deity with any other."

Abram opened his arms wide and bellowed to the courtroom. "Don't you see? I am the only omnipotent god. No one is more powerful." He stumbled a couple of steps backward and leaned against a doorframe. Abram hissed, "Your research has uncovered only a tiny glimpse of my plans and my power." His voice cracked, and he bent forward at the waist. "Even if Matt and I vanished today, the plan is already in motion with thousands of moving parts. Thousands—" He wheezed in and out, struggling to breathe. "Nothing you do will stop it. It will not be stopped by you or ..." His voice faded and his knees buckled. Abram slid to the floor with a thud.

"What did you do?" Matt yelled.

Eliana knelt by Abram. "I didn't do anything. Call an ambulance." She checked his wrists and neck for a nonexistent pulse.

Matt backed up and covered his mouth. "You … killed … him. Call your own ambulance." He looked around the room and fixed his eyes on an exit.

"Matt, please reconsider before it's too late."

Matt rushed out through one of the justice dressing rooms without looking back.

~~

One month later

Eliana phoned Julie. "Hi, Julie. How are you?"

"Hello, 'Miss in-the-News Barrington.' You're quite in demand on the networks."

Eliana laughed. "Well, not all the networks."

"Even so, the cell phone videos of you by the bronze doors have gone viral. How are you?"

"I'm doing well. How are you?"

"Great. I love the online Bible study. It's so good to see you there, even if you aren't using your real name."

"I'm so proud of all you're doing in the online course. It thrills my heart to see how much you're learning and growing. How are Emma and Todd?"

"We're all doing really well. Todd and I have also joined a local Bible study group. Looking back, I knew something was missing in my life, but I never realized it was God. Every day I'm amazed at how much I needed this, how much I needed Him. We found a good church. The people in the congregation have welcomed us and taken us in. They treat us like family."

"And how is Todd doing?"

"He's using his woodworking skills to help some of the people in the church. After the fire, he was despondent over the loss of so many pieces of furniture he'd made through the years. Woodworking had been his sole means of relaxing and distracting himself when the PTSD hit him so hard. I was afraid he would blame God and sink into another pit of depression and anger. You saw a little of that at the hospital. But after we joined the Bible study and church, he started using his woodworking skills to help other people. Todd builds ramps and things like that, and he also carves small crosses and gives them to people."

"Sounds like you are both blessed and blessing others. What about Emma?"

Julie giggled. "Our Emma's great. If you hear someone squealing in the background, that's her. We're outside and a butterfly keeps landing on her hand. She's dancing around in the sunshine, and this little butterfly is staying with her."

Eliana asked, "Is it yellow, by chance?"

"It is. It is so precious to watch. I wish I had my camera. She's talking to it like a friend."

Someday I'll have to tell her that story.

Julie continued, "It's amazing how God has met our every need and given our family such peace and contentment. Emma loves to talk about meeting Jesus and her little brother in Heaven. Her recovery, Todd's new attitude, the peace within our family—it's all truly astonishing."

"I am so happy for you."

"I'm going into the office every day, even with no justice there at the moment. A lot of rumors are floating around about who the president will pick to take his place. We'll have to wait and see. Any idea what happened to Matt after your meeting with him and Abram? Have any idea where he might be hiding?"

"None. He and his family have a lot of resources. He's probably overseas somewhere. Even with all the indictments, his family have hidden their assets, I'm sure."

"Your information exposed a lot of their criminal activity. They will be in litigation for some time. How are you? I was really sorry to hear about the death of Mrs. Moore, your grandmother."

"Thank you. I miss her terribly, but I know she is happy to be with the Lord. One of Grandma's favorite caretakers used to tell me 'her and the Good Lord, they have it all worked out.' I believe that. I believe that she and Granddaddy are together in the presence of God now. I look forward to joining them one day. And I'm glad you have her pearls."

"I will cherish them for as long as I live."

"When my granddaddy gave them to Grandma on their wedding day, she told him they were far too extravagant a gift. He told her, 'But ours is an extravagant love.' How could she refuse them after that?"

"Then they went to your mother?"

"Yes, and when she had them, she used to use them as an object lesson. Of course, oysters produce pearls when a grain of sand or some other irritant, gets between the mantle and the shell. Like the oyster had a splinter. It can't pull out the splinter, but it can cover it. So, layers and layers of covering produce the pearl. Without the pain, there is no pearl. God can use the difficult times in our lives to make something beautiful."

"Eliana, that makes perfect sense. A lovely way to explain it."

"I hope the pearls remind you of all that. The extravagant gift of love God has for you, the process of enduring hardships knowing that God can make something beautiful from them, and of my ongoing prayers for you."

"I know you're incognito most of the time, but I hope we can keep in touch."

"Me too. I can't wait to hear more about how your relationship with God is growing. I wouldn't be surprised to hear one day that you accomplished twice as much as I did there. I'm still moving around a lot and using throw-away phones, but I'll check in when I can and send you a new email address. You can leave me messages and someone will send them to me. I don't know where God will put me next, and I can't risk staying with my mom and brother."

"Be careful. I'm so thankful God put you here to reach me. Really. I don't know where I'd be without all you've done for me."

"I'm glad you will carry on there. Maybe your influence will touch Shally, Kirstie, and Ron. They need to know God but are still so blinded. I pray God will soften their hearts so they will be receptive to Him."

"Shally is asking questions. She told me about the day she visited you, right before the meeting with Abram. She wondered how you could be so calm, knowing Abram was out for your head. That gave me a chance to talk about God and the peace He has given me. I've invited her to join the online Bible study and she's popped in a couple of times. Shally's started using her full name, too, Shalom."

"That's encouraging. See God is already using you."

"The way you faced danger with such courage will always inspire me. You confronted Abram and Matt, knowing what they were capable of and what they had already done, but you did it anyway. I kind of expected to be going to your funeral. Instead, it was Abram's funeral that took place."

"God didn't promise me I would come out alive. But right before all that happened, I found—correction, God put in front of me—a bookmark that Mom had in her Bible. On one side it had my name, Eliana, and the meaning, *My God Answered*. The other side had *Elijah, My God is YHWH* on it, and a passage from Ephesians, chapter six."

"The armor of God?"

"Exactly."

"Our Bible study leader has encouraged us to memorize that passage."

"That's good advice. Being strong comes from the Lord. We need His armor head to toe to stand firm against evil."

"That's right. Before I confronted Abram, I armed myself with that and followed what God told me to do. He didn't say go when it was convenient or when I thought it was safe. He didn't even promise me that I would live through it. My eternity with Him was settled, so leaving this life on earth was no problem for me—*absent from the body, present with the Lord*. It was, and still is, more important to obey Him even when it might cost my life than to try and preserve my life.

His mandate to Elijah, then to the disciples and us, was to go, make disciples, and teach them. When He said go, I went."

"I'm thankful you did survive."

"I am too. I'll still be working online with Bible studies. I'm also mentoring some small Christian groups of people who want to be ready to take action against the foundation and the satellite groups around it. Even if I can't personally be in touch with you often, I will pray for you. Listen for Him and obey Him, no matter what."

"I will. And I will wear my pearls every day. I'm counting on those prayers."

"You have them, my friend. My God answers."

~~

The Elijah Mandate

Lisa Worthey Smith

Scripture referenced in the story

I included references to these Scriptures in the story because they have brought me strength through the years. If you are persecuted, weary, alone, or discouraged, I pray these powerful passages will bring you a refreshed hope and strength as they did to Eliana and to me.

For the story of Elijah, read 1 Kings and 2 Kings.

Other references to the Word of God within the story are listed below using NASB.

Chapter 3

2 Corinthians 12:9a "And He has said to me, "My grace is sufficient for you, for power is perfected in weakness.""

Exodus 8:21-24 "For if you do not let My people go, behold, I will send swarms of flies on you and on your servants and on your people and into your houses; and the houses of the Egyptians will be full of swarms of flies, and also the ground on which they dwell. "But on that day I will set apart (*palah*) the land of Goshen, where My people are living, so that no swarms of flies will be there, in order that you may know that I, the LORD, am in the midst of the land. "I will put a division (*peduwth*) between My people and your people. Tomorrow this sign will occur."" Then the LORD did so. And there came great swarms of flies into the house of Pharaoh and the houses of his servants and the land was laid waste because of the swarms of flies in all the land of Egypt."

1 Corinthians 15:51-52 "Behold, I tell you a mystery; we will not all sleep, but we will all be changed, in a moment, in the twinkling of an

eye, at the last trumpet; for the trumpet will sound, and the dead will be raised imperishable, and we will be changed."

1 Corinthians 15:55-58 "O DEATH, WHERE IS YOUR VICTORY? O DEATH, WHERE IS YOUR STING? The sting of death is sin, and the power of sin is the law; but thanks be to God, who gives us the victory through our Lord Jesus Christ. Therefore, my beloved brethren, be steadfast, immovable, always abounding in the work of the Lord, knowing that your toil is not in vain in the Lord."

Chapter 4

Psalm 34:7 "The angel of the LORD encamps around those who fear Him, and rescues them."

Chapter 7

Esther 4:14 "For if you remain silent at this time, relief and deliverance will arise for the Jews from another place and you and your father's house will perish. And who knows whether you have not attained royalty for such a time as this?"

Chapter 9

Deuteronomy 20:3,4 "He shall say to them, 'Hear, O Israel, you are approaching the battle against your enemies today. Do not be fainthearted. Do not be afraid, or panic, or tremble before them, for the LORD your God is the one who goes with you, to fight for you against your enemies, to save you.'"

2 Samuel 22:3,4 "My God, my rock, in whom I take refuge, my shield and the horn of my salvation, my stronghold and my refuge; my savior, You save me from violence. "I call upon the LORD, who is worthy to be praised, and I am saved from my enemies."

Psalm 138:7 "Though I walk in the midst of trouble, You will revive me; You will stretch forth Your hand against the wrath of my enemies, and Your right hand will save me."

2 Corinthians 4:7-9 "But we have this treasure in earthen vessels, so that the surpassing greatness of the power will be of God and not from ourselves; we are afflicted in every way, but not crushed; perplexed, but not despairing; persecuted, but not forsaken; struck down, but not destroyed;"

Hebrews 13:6 "so that we confidently say, "THE LORD IS MY HELPER, I WILL NOT BE AFRAID. WHAT WILL MAN DO TO ME?"

Ephesians 6:10-17 "Finally, be strong in the Lord and in the strength of His might. Put on the full armor of God, so that you will be able to stand firm against the schemes of the devil. For our struggle is not against flesh and blood, but against the rulers, against the powers, against the world forces of this darkness, against the spiritual forces of wickedness in the heavenly places. Therefore, take up the full armor of God, so that you will be able to resist in the evil day, and having done everything, to stand firm. Stand firm therefore, HAVING GIRDED YOUR LOINS WITH TRUTH, and HAVING PUT ON THE BREASTPLATE OF RIGHTEOUSNESS, and having shod YOUR FEET WITH THE PREPARATION OF THE GOSPEL OF PEACE; in addition to all, taking up the shield of faith with which you will be able to extinguish all the flaming arrows of the evil one. And take THE HELMET OF SALVATION, and the sword of the Spirit, which is the word of God."

Chapter 10

John 21:15-17 "So when they had finished breakfast, Jesus said to Simon Peter, "Simon, son of John, do you love Me more than these?" He said to Him, "Yes, Lord; You know that I love You." He said to him, "Tend My lambs." He said to him again a second time, "Simon, son of John, do you love Me?" He said to Him, "Yes, Lord; You know that I love You." He said to him, "Shepherd My sheep." He said to him the third time, "Simon, son of John, do you love Me?" Peter was grieved because He said to him the third time, "Do you love Me?" And he said to Him, "Lord, You know all things; You know that I love You." Jesus said to him, "Tend My sheep."

Chapter 11

Ephesians 2:8 "For by grace you have been saved through faith; and that not of yourselves, it is the gift of God;"

Chapter 13

Jeremiah 10:11-13 "Thus you shall say to them, "The gods that did not make the heavens and the earth will perish from the earth and from under the heavens." It is He who made the earth by His power, Who established the world by His wisdom; and by His understanding He has stretched out the heavens. When He utters His voice, there is a tumult of waters in the heavens, and He causes the clouds to ascend from the end of the earth; He makes lightning for the rain, and brings out the wind from His storehouses."

Philippians 4:6,7 "Be anxious for nothing, but in everything by prayer and supplication with thanksgiving let your requests be made known to God, and the peace of God, which surpasses all comprehension, will guard your hearts and your minds in Christ Jesus."

Revelation 3:7b "He who is holy, who is true, who has the key of David, who opens and no one will shut, and who shuts and no one opens."

Daniel 2:21 "It is He who changes the times and the epochs; He removes kings and establishes kings; He gives wisdom to wise men and knowledge to men of understanding."

Ephesians 6:12 "For our struggle is not against flesh and blood, but against the rulers, against the powers, against the world forces of this darkness, against the spiritual forces of wickedness in the heavenly places."

2 Kings 19:35 "Then it happened that night that the angel of the LORD went out and struck 185,000 in the camp of the Assyrians; and when men rose early in the morning, behold, all of them were dead."

2 Kings 2:9 "When they had crossed over, Elijah said to Elisha, "Ask what I shall do for you before I am taken from you." And Elisha said, "Please, let a double portion of your spirit be upon me."

Note ~

Elisha's ministry lasted twice as long as Elijah's.

God used Elijah to perform eight miracles, Elisha sixteen.

Elijah's eight Miracles (1 Kings and 2 Kings)

1. Shut out rain from heaven (1 Kings 17:1).
2. Flour and oil jars never emptied (1 Kings 17:14).
3. Widow's son raised (1 Kings 17:22-23).
4. Fire from heaven that consumed sacrifice (1 Kings 18:38).
5. Rain after drought (1 Kings 18:45).
6. Fire consumed fifty men plus captain (2 Kings 1:10).
7. Fire consumed fifty men plus captain (2 Kings 1:12).
8. Divided Jordan (2 Kings 2:8).

Elisha's sixteen miracles 2 Kings

1. Divided Jordan (2 Kings 2:14).
2. Cleansed water (2 Kings 2:21).
3. Bears killed those who mocked him (2 Kings 2:24).
4. Water in trenches (2 Kings 3:13-20).
5. Increased the supply of oil for widow (2 Kings 4:1-6).
6. Son for old woman (2 Kings 4:16-17).
7. Raised Shunammite son (2 Kings 4:36).
8. Cleansed food in pot from poisonous herb (2 Kings 4:41).
9. Bread multiplied to feed many (2 Kings 4:43).
10. Healed Naaman from leprosy (2 Kings 5:10).

11. Gehazi smitten (2 Kings 5:27).
12. Iron axe head floated, saved a man from ruin (2 Kings 6:6).
13. Gave sight to blind (2 Kings 6:17).
14. Struck people with blindness (2 Kings 6:18)
15. Restored sight (2 Kings 6:20).
16. Dead man came alive when buried atop Elisha's bones. (2 Kings 13:21).

2 Corinthians 5:6-8 "Therefore, being always of good courage, and knowing that while we are at home in the body we are absent from the Lord—for we walk by faith, not by sight. Be are of good courage, I say, and prefer rather to be absent from the body and to be at home with the Lord."

Matthew 28:18-20 "And Jesus came up and spoke to them, saying, "All authority has been given to Me in heaven and on earth. Go therefore and make disciples of all the nations, baptizing them in the name of the Father and the Son and the Holy Spirit, teaching them to observe all that I commanded you; and lo, I am with you always, even to the end of the age."

About the author

Multiple award-winning and bestselling author, Lisa Worthey Smith, weaves stories brimming with faith, hope, and love. She draws from her many years as a Bible student and Bible study leader for both profound and simple layers that add spiritual depth to the canvas. Her passion is sharing biblical truths in such a way that readers gain a fresh understanding of how the Word of God is relevant to their lives.

Lisa and her high school sweetheart husband are empty-nesting in north Alabama where she serves as president of North Alabama Word Weavers, tends her hummingbird garden, and tippy taps on her keyboard with a cup of Earl Grey beside her.

Your reviews help potential readers know if a book is right for them, and make the book more visible. If you enjoyed The Elijah Mandate, please consider leaving a brief, honest review on Amazon.

Blessings,

Lisa Worthey Smith

Other books by Lisa Worthey Smith

Unsung Heroes
The Vietnam War casualties and facts we forgot to remember. Why that time remains relevant to us today.

COFFEE with God,
Collection of devotions by North Alabama Word Weavers

The Ground Kisser,
Multiple award-winning. The Vietnam War story you haven't heard through the eyes of a young girl you won't forget. A patriotic look at America through the eyes of a grateful immigrant.

The Wisdom Tree
An ordinary olive tree in the garden of Gethsemane who witnessed an extraordinary time in history. Bible study included.

Oscar the Extraordinary Hummingbird
Reader voted top 50 indie books worth reading. True story of a gravely injured hummingbird. Bible study included.

Lisa Worthey Smith

Made in USA - Kendallville, IN
1165360_9781734495461